'I enjoy a challe

Nathan continued, '
that. And, despite y
are as fascinated b
mistress as——'

'Lover,' Annie countered automatically in a
stunned voice. 'You accuse me of being an
amoral opportunist and in the next breath
proposition me. What does that make you?'

His eyes, smoky green, were examining her
with all the warmth of a microscope lens.

'Why are you so scared of me, Annie?'

Kim Lawrence lives on a farm in rural Anglesey. She runs two miles daily and finds this an excellent opportunity to unwind and seek inspiration for her writing! It also helps her keep up with her husband, two active sons, and the various stray animals which have adopted them. Always a fanatical consumer of fiction, she is now equally enthusiastic about writing. She loves a happy ending!

Recent titles by the same author:

PASSIONATE RETRIBUTION

RELENTLESS
SEDUCTION

BY
KIM LAWRENCE

MILLS & BOON

*All the characters in this book have no existence outside the
imagination of the author, and have no relation whatsoever to anyone
bearing the same name or names. They are not even distantly inspired
by any individual known or unknown to the author, and all the
incidents are pure invention.*

*MILLS & BOON and the Rose Device
are trademarks of the publisher.
Harlequin Mills & Boon Limited,
Eton House, 18–24 Paradise Road, Richmond, Surrey TW9 1SR*

© Kim Lawrence 1995

ISBN 0 263 79386 9

*Set in 10 on 10½ pt Linotron Times
01-9602-59441*

*Typeset in Great Britain by CentraCet, Cambridge
Made and printed in Great Britain*

CHAPTER ONE

THE anticipated shock of icy water came. Breath caught in a silent cry in her throat, Annie surfaced alongside her swimming companion. Water streaming down her face, she wiped at the thick strands of waterlogged hair that obstructed her view; usually coppery red, they had been turned to dark rust by the immersion.

'Isn't this glorious?'

Annie's generous mouth curved into an ironic smile. 'You think so?' she said, looking into an exuberant, tanned face. With his dark hair slicked back Josh looked remarkably like an otter, an analogy which seemed even more apt as his supple, streamlined body struck out, cleaving through the water, leaving only a war cry of triumph in the afternoon air.

Indulgently and with considerably less speed she followed his example. It was either that or freeze to death; the late May sun might have been giving an illusion of Mediterranean heat, but the unheated pool made it quite clear that this was England and tomorrow might well give arctic conditions.

Squinting against the sun, she rolled on to her back and slowly traversed the pool. It was a pleasant sensation and she was glad she'd allowed herself to be dragged away from her books. Perhaps Josh was right; she had been working hard; even so, the finals were looming closer and she needed to do well, not just for her own sake—she owed it to David.

Dreamily she began to drift until her idyll was ruined by Josh, who unceremoniously dragged her under. She retaliated in turn and a noisy, breathless fight ensued. Eventually she admitted defeat and laughingly swam to the edge of the pool.

Arms and legs perhaps too unused to such physical exertion of late refused to obey her commands to lever herself free of the water. About to turn to Josh and demand a leg up, she was startled when a hand grasped her wrist and effortlessly, or so it seemed, pulled her clear of the water.

She stood, water streaming off her pale, slim body, silhouetted in the plain black swimsuit she wore. Questioning, her clear grey eyes focused on the owner of the hands which still gripped her wrists. She was confused to find a stranger intruding on the privacy of Chausey. If she'd been alone, the thanks and unconscious warm smile that curved her full lips might not have been so spontaneous; but she was aware of Josh's presence and could afford to be uninhibited in her natural response.

'Good afternoon,' she said, lifting the hand that had been released to shade her eyes from the direct glare of the sun. 'And thank you; I must be out of condition,' she added ruefully, her eyes flicking to the long curve of her thighs. Her nose in books, she'd neglected exercise of late. Deciding that she must do something about this as soon as the finals were over, she returned her attention to her visitor. 'Can I help?' she began.

He moved to one side and for the first time she could see him clearly. The dark outline which had seemed simply bulky as a shadow against the glare became leaner but equally tall and broad of shoulder, which had given her the false impression of grossness for a fleeting instant.

Clad in a formal dark suit and dazzling white shirt which made no concessions to the heat, this was the body of a man who couldn't disguise his steely strength even with the ultra-sleek tailoring. She strongly doubted whether the fine, lightweight cloth had been cut to disguise any surplus flesh; he gave the impression of smooth, controlled strength.

So much unmuted masculine power was, on some

level of her consciousness, rather like an assault. Registering this and surprise at her own nebulous discomfort, her eyes hurriedly rose beyond the shirt collar.

For a split-second she felt as if her body had stopped functioning; her senses had been jolted into a state of suspended animation. She recovered quickly, only a widening of her clear grey eyes, a flickering of her sooty lashes and a certain tautness in her oval face betraying the momentary sensation.

Foolish, really; she'd seen good-looking men before and hadn't suffered such an electrifying reaction— although none, perhaps, she conceded, had been endowed with such a concentrated beauty, perfect bone-structure, peculiarly, startlingly green eyes and a mouth that was a miracle of sensuality.

'Possibly.'

Annie looked startled, not really by the oddly oblique reply but because the voice wasn't the smooth, bland tone she'd expected; it was gravelly, very deep, and overly familiar to her sensitive ears. She felt herself bridle; her wearing a swimsuit gave no man the right to examine her as though she'd arrayed herself specially for his approval, and there was a certain cynical appreciation in the absinthe-coloured eyes which were overtly exploring her body.

'Your condition looks quite good to me,' he continued casually.

She met the green eyes, which were analysing her angry reaction with a degree of gleaming humour that faded, leaving only an expression which was distinctly unsettling. She gave a sigh of relief when Josh chose that moment to lever himself out of the pool. He shook his head, sending a flurry of icy droplets into the immediate area. She flinched as several struck her skin which was already growing warm beneath the sun's rays.

Josh's attention was only on the guest for a split-second before he gave a sudden cry of welcome, looking beyond her; and as he moved forward Annie saw the familiar, lanky figure of her stepson hurrying over the terrace.

The two men exchanged hearty slaps on the shoulder which she knew was meant to demonstrate a friendship which had lasted all their lives and would only deepen with time. Her turn came and her stepson Matthew Selby delivered a kiss that landed somewhere west of her left ear, and then he placed her at arm's length.

'Are you feeding yourself?' he asked, a critical frown deepening between his brows, making the spectacles slip lower over the bridge of his nose.

Annie felt laughter tug at the corners of her mouth. Somewhere along the way the parent-son relationship had got sadly muddled, but considering that Matthew was two years her senior this was hardly surprising. She felt a sharp stab of pleasure as she smiled with deep affection at the gangly young man whose legs appeared to go on forever. Their friendship was a permanent legacy of her marriage and one which she valued more than most things in life.

He could have resented her—the girl he'd known most of his life who'd suddenly married his father; but, although he'd disapproved of the union and hadn't pretended otherwise, he had been a tower of strength when she'd needed someone.

'Blame the emaciation on my metabolic-rate,' she said solemnly. While she was certainly slender, nothing could have looked less emaciated than her somewhat lush curves, and in the swimsuit, her attributes were in no way disguised.

'You're wet,' he continued in an aggrieved tone as he regarded the dark stains on his suit—a dark suit, like the stranger's, though Matthew's was typically creased and his tie was askew. Annie quelled an instinct to straighten it and waited for some explanation. The stranger's presence must be linked with his, she reasoned, aware of the unblinking regard of the green eyes.

The profile, carved from stone and too rigid to be spontaneous, turned to regard Matthew; the jaw, rock-hard and angular, tightened and she watched the play of muscle and sinew along the column of his throat.

'I see you've met Nathan,' Matthew added. 'I've been combing the house searching for you.'

She had a name to fit the face—a face that rattled her almost as much as its owner did. The fact irritated her; she was rarely intimidated by anyone.

'I persuaded Annie to take a break. The one person I know who doesn't need to cram and she's entered some self-imposed purdah.' With casual affection Josh patted her behind. 'All this brain work goes straight to the hips, sweetheart.'

Annie twisted her head and poked her tongue out at Josh, drawing a quick laugh from the two younger men and sneering disdain from the older, mystery man. His outright contempt, of which she caught a fleeting glimpse, was offensive and peculiar. What had she done to deserve that? she puzzled, doing her best to ignore the definite insult and trying to keep a firm rein on the anger which was beginning to build up inside her suddenly tight chest.

'Leave me to worry about my hips,' she responded drily. Josh insulted her with the ease of long acquaint-ance. He was a contemporary of Matthew's and she knew the task of 'keeping an eye on Annie' had fallen to him. It was a situation she tolerated because he wasn't heavy-handed and at times it was pleasant to have an undemanding companion, especially when the attendance of a male saved her from unwanted attentions.

'Actually, Matthew, we haven't been introduced,' she said, her eyes seeking an explanation.

'I thought. . . Sorry, love. This is Nathan Audley,' he announced with a flourish. 'This is Annie Selby.'

Annie's eyes widened. This was Matthew's boss, the elusive entrepreneur who numbered among his numerous possessions the string of international hotels that Matthew had gone to work for directly from university. This had disappointed his father who had wanted his offspring to follow in his illustrious, academic footsteps.

Age had not proved a barrier to Matthew's somewhat meteoric rise through the echelons and Annie, aware that the forgetful, bespectacled look had been formulated in the days when he had been embarrassed by his own intellect, was pleased rather than surprised. Still, the big boss himself in tow; she was impressed.

'How nice.' She pinned a smile on her lips, unwilling to allow her newly born but strong antipathy to embarrass her stepson. Her hand was taken in a cool, firm grip and she was relieved when the contact was broken. There were calluses on the palm of the manicured hands; she wondered why she was cataloguing such minute details. 'If you'd like to come indoors I'll rustle up some tea.'

He was not what she had imagined. . .far younger. The sophisticated air he carried with him was counterbalanced by a certain indefinable vitality and power. This man was a power broker, she reminded herself. It did explain the air of superiority and the arrogance. He obviously took his own press releases too seriously, she thought derisively, determined not to be impressed.

She caught up her wrap from the weed-encrusted paving at the same moment as Nathan Audley did. After a brief and undignified tussle she released the garment and allowed it to be placed across her shoulders. Twin flags of colour bloomed in the uniform pallor of her creamy, matt complexion.

'How kind,' she muttered, aware that her tone implied the opposite and Matthew had shot her a look of surprise.

'I must love you and leave you, folks. Got a seminar in an hour,' Josh announced in his usual breezy style.

He nodded at Nathan, slapped Matthew on the back and kissed Annie in a friendly manner which she reciprocated.

She linked her arm with Matthew's and reprimanded him in a fierce undertone, 'You might have warned me.'

'Predictability isn't Nathan's strong point, Annie; I didn't even——'

'This must be an attractive garden when it isn't so neglected.' The indolent observation interrupted the hurried tête-à-tête and Annie stumbled over a loose flagstone.

'Help is so difficult to get nowadays,' she responded gravely; her smile flashed out brilliantly and insincerely. She was all too well aware of how much work the rambling property needed but being reminded of it by this man made her grit her teeth.

The sudden gleam in the green eyes betrayed a humour that she would have been happier to believe he didn't possess.

'Do you have a large staff, Mrs Selby?'

'Considering I'm the only occupant, Mr Audley, a large staff would be over-indulgent.'

'Might help the weed problem, though, Mrs Selby,' he replied blandly, standing aside to allow her to enter the doorway before him. 'To be honest, I was thinking more of the fabric of the building than your comfort; I feel sure that you are more than capable of taking whatever measures you deem necessary in that area.'

The insult was issued in such a matter-of-fact, almost congratulatory fashion that for a split-second she thought she must have misheard. One glimpse of the contempt in the hard green gaze dispelled this illusion. The antipathy she felt was obviously returned with interest. She tilted her chin and willed her face to register indifference to the uninformed disapproval levelled at her, a practice she'd perfected some time before.

'Take Nathan into the drawing-room, Annie; I'll organise some tea.'

Matthew hadn't been privy to his employer's soft-voiced insults, she realised—a fact made obvious by his 'isn't this cosy?' expression. She stared after him in frustration and grudgingly led the way into the drawing-room.

None of the rooms at Chausey was vast; that was part of the charm of the old manor house. This south-facing parlour was delightful—part of the original Elizabethan building. The stone-mullioned, lead-latticed windows were flung open, letting the sweet smells that wafted in from the old-fashioned cottage garden mingle with the scent of lovingly waxed wood and pot-pourri, which spilled from the delicate china containers. It was the one room she tried to keep in the condition it deserved, giving it the same loving care which had once been lavished upon the whole house.

No doubt this man would turn up his superior nose at the faded curtains and original tapestry that upholstered the chairs. Stiffly she nodded him to a seat. 'If you'll excuse me, I'll get dressed.' Her fingers smoothed the fabric of her robe while her brain objected to the fact that her visitor was subjecting her to the same piercing scrutiny as he had given the room, as though he were assessing a possible acquisition, she thought with distaste.

'Not on my account.' One dark brow raised slowly and eloquently.

'Hardly,' she began. She bit her lower lip to repress any further indiscreet remarks. This man was important to Matthew, she reminded herself. She didn't have to like him, just tolerate him for a brief time. That shouldn't stretch her too far... Oddly enough it did. 'As Matthew pointed out, I'm wet.'

He inclined his head, the gesture impatient, dismissive, as though his tolerance had worn paper-thin. 'Matthew speaks highly of you...dotingly,' he sneered.

'He didn't mention that you're one of those fortunate women who look better with their clothes off. You must be extremely bright,' he added, ignoring her swift inhalation of shock. Heavy lids half shaded the grim green gaze and he stretched his long legs in front of him and leaned deeper into the sofa.

Annie felt as if she was being interviewed—or, rather, interrogated, she corrected herself. She had the strangest sensation—rather like walking into the middle of a conversation and feeling unsure of what had gone before.

'You think Matthew admires my intelligence or my ability to strip?' she asked with ironic interest. A frown appeared to flaw the smooth perfection of her wide brow; it was the only external indicator of her feelings as she sought to hide her reaction to his comments.

She decided to sit, partly because her knees were showing a tendency to buckle. The intensity of this man, even when he was making some mundane comment, was stressful, daunting. Was he trying to provoke her, or was this his normal form of small talk? she wondered angrily. Did he consider it his right to be as insulting as was conceivable?

'What I mean, Mrs Selby, is that to make Matthew think well of you you must have, at the very least, native cunning to match your abundant if obvious physical attributes.'

The swift inhalation swelled the 'attributes' he had smilingly referred to. Wrath mingled with disbelief; the overt offensiveness was staggering. The green gaze had sunk lower to her legs—long and slim, folded neatly at the ankle—and a sound of fury escaped from her throat.

One dark eyebrow quirked expressively. 'Do you have a problem?'

'Suppose you tell me what *your* problem is? Because you might be Matthew's boss but there are limits to what I'm prepared to endure even for him.' She breathed deeply in an attempt to contain her temper.

'Of course, Matthew is your meal ticket, isn't he? It wouldn't do if he lost his income.'

She let the first sneering comment pass; the second bothered her too much. This man wasn't really capable of actually dismissing Matthew, was he? she wondered incredulously. Just because she couldn't endure his bizarre line in insults? 'I feel sure that, working for you, he earns every penny,' she retorted.

'And you spend it.'

That stunned her; She had never accepted a penny from Matthew. In fact, she insisted on paying her fair share of the maintenance on the house even though it was eating into the money David had left her; her part-time job at the nursery school was hardly financially rewarding.

'I fail to see what my finances have to do with you,' she said coldly. She shivered and gathered the material closer around herself.

'Then I'll be frank, shall I?' His chiselled, angular features adopted an infuriating, patronising smugness. 'I want something, Mrs Selby, and you are in the way. I remove obstacles, whatever form they take; you are an obstacle, and, as such, I take a great interest in everything about you,' he observed dispassionately.

Something akin to panic was building up inside her skull. Was this man totally mad? He was dangerous—she could see that. It was in his eyes—a relentless implacability. 'I've not the faintest idea what you're talking about.'

'I want to buy Chausey, Annie.' He spoke her name as if he were tasting it; the sound made her stomach muscles clench in protest.

She stared at him. 'Chausey isn't for sale.'

'That is a very naïve thing for you of all people to say. Isn't there always a price? I mean, didn't you pay to live here? It must have been so frustrating for you when the old man left it to Matthew,' he goaded. 'Still,' he added judiciously. 'I admire the fact that you made the best of a bad job. You still manage to freeload and play lady of the manor, and entertain as many young studs as you please.'

The vase hadn't been genuine—she recalled the valuers pointing that out when the estate had been settled—but it was very pretty. And it was a shame to waste such lovely early roses—she had only picked them earlier—but it was worth it to see Nathan Audley's face as the water soaked into his expensive Italian suit. Impulse could be so satisfying sometimes, she decided.

His epithet was to the point, his jaw rigid as he clamped his lips over further comment. The anger that spilled from his eyes as they swivelled in her direction was snuffed out with confusing precision. Annie shivered suddenly; it amazed her that someone with such obviously violent emotions could exert so much control in disguising them. 'I hope you enjoyed doing that,' he said, with a casualness she found vaguely disturbing.

'I did,' she confirmed. He had insulted her more in the space of minutes than anyone had in her entire life. She was literally shaking with rage; her teeth jarred against one another spasmodically.

'Remember that when you're paying for it.'

'I'm trembling with anticipation,' she assured him, widening her eyes to their fullest extent; she was trembling all right—it was all she could do to disguise the fact. Her mind was in total disorder. Matthew would never sell Chausey. She loved every mellow stone of the place, every inconvenient, draughty nook. Did Matthew? The unbidden thought surfaced only to be firmly repressed.

'I know I'm supposed to be awestruck by your masterful, boorish tactics but I was never impressed by spoilt little boys used to getting their own way, and I'm still not, no matter what age they happen to be.

Chausey, Mr Audley, is not for sale, and even if it were you'd be the last person I'd sell it to.'

The very idea of the place falling into the hands of a man with all the soul of a computer chip made her skin crawl. She threw back her head, sending her hair, which had begun to dry into its usual rippling mass of curls, whipping about her face. Her eyes were clear slate-grey, cold and dismissive.

Nathan's eyes were fixed on her face unblinkingly, the expression in them hard to decipher. 'But Chausey isn't yours to sell,' he said softly.

This timely reminder made her flush; a deep car-nation colour stained the smooth contours of her cheeks and she felt the heat travel down the column of her throat. The trouble was that though she had never owned Chausey her bond with the house had grown so strong over the years that she had a habit of overlook-ing the fact.

As a child she'd lived with her aunt at the gatehouse; Aunt Mirrie had cooked for the family—not a difficult task with Matthew away at prep school and his father forever on guest tours of the States or supervising digs in various inaccessible parts of the globe.

The place had been hers to explore, and had been an early fascination which had deepened. Later, of course, she'd been mistress of the house; but that time had been brief and there had been too much pain associated with it for her to recall the one time she had had a legitimate claim to Chausey with pleasure.

'I have the right to live here,' she defended herself, tight-lipped. A strange sensation feathered through the pit of her stomach as he stood up, brushing the damp foliage from his clothes with fastidious distaste. Her mind traced the unpleasant sensation to its source and she blinked away a momentary confusion. It was the way he moved—smoothly, with an almost feline co-ordination that exposed rather than concealed the power in his tall frame.

She restrained the impulse to take a step backwards
and retreat from the threat that was somehow implicit
in his physical presence. 'The will specified that
Chausey is my home as long as I wish, or until I marry.
Matthew can't sell while I'm here. He couldn't stomach
having you turn his home into a hotel. He feels very
strongly about his family history.'

Her lip curled with distaste and her voice trembled
with condemnation. The very idea of her beloved
Chausey becoming another acquisition in this man's
empire, reduced to a column of figures on some financial ledger, hijacked the remnants of her discretion. She
wanted to physically remove that smug sneer from this
man's face.

'I think you mean that you couldn't stomach having
Matt turf you out on your delectable butt. Mrs Selby is
having far too much fun playing the field to marry, isn't
she, sweetheart?' The green eyes held a lofty disdain
that made her teeth grate together. In less fraught
circumstances she might almost have smiled at the
irony of this supposition. 'How old were you the first
time. . .nineteen?'

'Eighteen,' she corrected him coldly.

A dark brow quirked. 'Pardon me; eighteen,' he
drawled. 'If you were capable of such a pragmatic
decision at that tender age no doubt you'll behave
equally cannily the next time around. I expect you feel
you've earned a break from the grind of indulging an
elderly fool.'

There had been a time when she'd shied away from
these commonly held assumptions. The age-gap alone
had been enough to cause tongues to wag, but the
dissimilarity in their social stations, even in a day and
age when class distinctions had supposedly been obliterated, had made them both the target of malicious
tongues.

David had been better equipped than she to cope
with the difficult moments. Besides, his friends had not

unnaturally cast her in the role of gold-digger rather than him in the role of seducer; but she had learnt to disguise her insecurity behind a cool indifference which she'd heard referred to as sophistication, a fact which made her smile wryly.

'I doubt if my long-term plans are of much interest to you.'

'I told you, Annie, everything about you is of interest to me until I get what I want. You'd be surprised how much I know about you. Matthew doesn't need much encouragement to talk about you. Did it give you a thrill to have a father and son in love with you?'

'Matthew is like a brother to me,' she protested swiftly.

'And the guy in the pool is your uncle, no doubt. What a wide and varied family you must have.'

Annie blinked. The picture of herself as some sort of dangerous siren was bizarre. She doubted very much if anything she said would alter this man's preconceptions; and why, she asked herself, should she justify herself to him?

'As we've established I'm the most calculating, avaricious female ever to draw breath, it must also be self-evident that I've no intention of moving aside to let you buy Chausey. I'm very. . .comfortable here.'

She traced the outline of her lips with calculated provocation. He was going to rip the soul out of this lovely old home if he was given the opportunity. She felt dizzy with a strange and heady mixture of disgust, resolve and exhilaration. Her lovely eyes glittered with her determination to keep Chausey out of his hands.

His eyes narrowed. 'I had intended to offer you a financial inducement.' The supercilious smile flickered tauntingly across the sensually sculpted lips which for some reason her eyes were unwillingly drawn to repeatedly. 'Don't get excited, though, Annie; that was before I realised how wide of the mark Matthew's assessment of you was. Not that I was expecting the girl next door that poor, deluded Matt thinks of you as—a fragile flower in need of a protector.

'Women like you make me ill. I doubt you're capable of empathy with another living being—your own comfort will always be the only priority you have. . .and if you hurt anyone else maintaining that comfort what the hell?' he said in disgust.

She realised that she was trembling in reaction to his savage attack. 'Don't leave it there, just as it was getting interesting.' Her expression was derisive. 'I'd be just fascinated to learn more about women like me.' she allowed her voice to rise an octave and adopted a mocking, little-girl voice.

The green eyes narrowed to slits and he rocked back on his heels. 'An erotic little slut,' he said consideringly. 'You've been using men for as long as you can remember, probably from the moment you realised it was easier than actually working for what you want. Although sleeping with a man who'd be considered elderly even as your father might be considered quite a high price to pay for pampered indolence. You're selfish to the backbone, otherwise you'd never stay on when the place is bleeding Matthew dry.'

'And your motivations are purely altruistic, I suppose?' She thrust her clenched fists deep into the pockets of her robe—fists that wanted to wipe that sneer off his grimly perfect face. She wasn't going to dignify his comments by actually putting him straight on several points.

'Isn't Chausey a little on the small side for the Audley empire?' she went on. 'Or are you going to knock it down and build something with several hundred identical rooms?' Her beloved home was never going to fall into the clutches of this monster, she silently vowed. 'I care about Chausey; it's meant to be a home, not a soulless hotel,' she told him scathingly.

'Home?' he snorted. 'What would a grasping little tramp like you—unless we're talking wrecking—know about homes? You reduce everything to its bankable value and Chausey, despite its sorry state, has considerable value.

'You must have been ready to murder when the old man left it to Matt. Did he finally realise at the last just what you are?' he speculated, his eyes gem-hard. 'You don't like it when someone sees you for what you are, do you, Annie?' he suggested slowly, almost with relish, his eyes on her face. 'Sees you as I do.'

'I'd say your vision is as distorted as your warped view of life,' she retorted with heartfelt sincerity. It would be just like this man to resort to bribery—sweeteners, he probably called it, amoral and ruthless. She just hoped that Matthew hadn't been tainted by the unsavoury autocrat.

'This is the real Annie Selby, isn't it? A snarling little cat. Poor Matt, you're really taking him for a ride, aren't you?'

'You leave Matthew alone.' Suddenly she felt her eyes fill with tears. She blinked furiously to banish them but one fell like a solitary jewel over the curve of her cheek.

Nathan's eyes fixed on the point of moisture with an almost reluctant fascination before returning to the loathing in her eyes. 'I think it would be educational for Matt to see you as you are,' he announced reflectively. 'I doubt he'd be such a biddable landlord if the blinkers were off. It's a real talent being able to cry to order, but feminine tears don't distract me...just irritate.'

'Nothing you could do could come between Matthew and me,' she said triumphantly. She was on safe ground now; her relationship with Matthew was inviolate; nothing this hateful man implied could alter that. As for Matthew wanting her to leave, that was nonsense; this was her home...their home, even though he'd shown no signs of wishing to stay here. In fact, he often teased her for her strong affinity to the old place. One day his family would live here; it needed children.

She blinked away the desolate sensation that hit her and faced her aggressor, smilingly confident. She heard Matthew's whistling through the studded oak door which stood ajar and made a move to open it. The man would at least pretend to be civilised in front of her stepson, she realised with relief.

'What?' she spat furiously as, with amazing speed and agility, Nathan grabbed her arm and swung her towards him.

'I admire your confidence; I thought I might put it to the test.' His dark face loomed dizzily close. 'Besides, I owe you one for the flowers.'

She knew what was coming and mentally the words 'prepare to meet thy doom' appeared in neon lights. Hysteria welled in her throat but she willed herself not to struggle. She doubted whether he'd get a kick out of forcing a brutish kiss on a rag doll, and he was going to kiss her, she was convinced, as a last-ditch effort to display his masculine superiority and show Matthew the sort of entertaining she did in his home. Pathetic, really, and predictable.

Nathan Audley momentarily seemed immobilised by the small smile that suddenly curved her full pink lips. He could see the tracery of fine blood vessels in her eyelids as they fluttered but remained firmly shut. She stood there like some sacrificial victim, her weight slumped against the encircling arm that had hauled her towards him. The swooping, predatory movement of his head slowed as he moved to claim his retribution.

Annie, steeled for a brief, undignified onslaught, felt a moment's total astonishment at the firm but gentle touch of cool lips which was almost reassuring. Her eyes flickered open and her unfettered hands made fluttery gestures, clutching at empty air as if to find some support to wrench her clear of this subtle viol-ation of her senses.

Abruptly the transition came and she stepped into an open void—black, warm and insidiously seductive. At that instant a small, fierce moan vibrated in her throat and her hands moved with preconditioned ease into the dark, crisp hair on the nape of his neck. The kiss which had been teasing, exploratory but almost chaste escalated until her senses were filled with the warmth and taste of him, excited by the dominant strength of the stranger who held her. The alien, hard strength of him was erotically intoxicating.

She broke away eventually; time was impossible to estimate—it could only be measured by the turbulent thud of her heart against her ribs. He didn't resist her efforts. Pale and panting, she met the enigmatic emerald gaze, her eyes spitting fury and defiance.

'No need for the outraged innocence; Matt retreated some time ago,' he told her with cynical indifference.

Matthew! She'd forgotten; a fresh wave of humiliation washed over her. This man had insulted her, doubted her integrity and on top of that had made her react like some sexually indiscriminate little idiot. 'I think you're the most loathsome, conniving, egocentric——'

'You really are magnificent when you're aroused,' he interrupted in a tone normally reserved for reporting the weather. 'In a colourful, overblown sort of way.'

'Overblown?' She gulped. He was laughing at her, she realised. That had to be the supreme insult.

'I do arouse you, don't I?' He wasn't laughing now, but his expression was scything through her doomed tranquillity like a knife through butter.

The deep carnation colour that had flooded her cheeks seeped away as his words slowly penetrated. The pallor emphasised the size and magnificence of her eyes and drew his heavy-lidded gaze to the fullness of her trembling lips. 'The only thing you arouse in me is complete and total disgust,' she said, the contempt in her voice reserved partly for herself; that she possessed such primal instincts was shocking; that she'd chosen to discover it at this of all moments was disastrous.

'You really are used to getting your own way, aren't you, angel? It might just be character-building for you to interact with someone who doesn't roll over and beg every time you flutter your eyelashes.

'In my situation I come across numerous women whose main objective in life, like your own, is to catch a rich husband. I try to make it clear that I'm not on the market, but occasionally,' he conceded drily, 'there are benefits.'

The speculative curve to his lips made her work overtime on quelling a totally irrational surge of panic. It washed over her in great breathless waves, leaving a trembling weakness in its wake. 'Interact?' she snorted, pleased at the scorn she injected into the word. 'In your dreams, Mr Nathan Audley.

'Benefits! You're disgusting. . .coarse.' Her voice trembled with temper and she subdued the impulse to stamp her foot. 'Even a gold-digging little trollop like me has her standards to maintain!'

'Is your hair really that colour? You'd rival a New England autumn.' His eyes touched the burnished mass of curls that seethed about her shoulders as if they possessed an independent life of their own.

For one awful moment she thought he was actually going to catch it in his hand, let it slide through his long fingers. 'A witch like you on my right arm might make the most persistent prospective wifey think twice,' he mused.

As if a woman could be taken out and displayed like a shiny new car, she thought, her stomach clenching in disgust at the comment. . .or was it the thought of him touching her hair? The forbidden notion was ruthlessly quelled. She concentrated on the implication that her only role could ever be that of ornament.

'It's out of a bottle,' she lied. He wasn't listening to her at all, she thought wrathfully; he just wasn't programmed to treat her as a human being. 'I have been implanted with silicone in just about every place possible. I wear hair extensions, false eyelashes and have liposuction on a weekly basis,' she declared outrageously. 'Or I would if it would guarantee I never had to see you again.

'I realise the tragic life you suffer probably accounts for your lack of personality. . .pursued by women all desperate to be your willing slaves.'

Her sympathy was ladled on with deep insincerity. His bark of laughter which rumbled forth at the height of her scornful diatribe was intensely infuriating. . .so much for insulting him—the appalling man was enjoying it! He had the hide of a rhino.

'Next time Matthew decides to entertain the boss, tell him to warn me so I can be elsewhere.' Slamming the door was childish but intensely satisfying. She took the bare wooden stairs two at a time, muttering furiously under her breath as she did so.

With a shuddering sigh of relief she closed her bedroom door and leaned against it; she was trembling with reaction. Her bodily functions all seemed to be working erratically, not just her weak and insubstantial knees. Where had been her discrimination, her self-respect downstairs? She'd kissed him back with more enthusiasm than she cared to recall in detail. With a small moan she flung herself headlong on her bed.

'Stupid. . .stupid. . .stupid.' Each word was punctuated by her fist hammering the defenceless pillow. She couldn't remember ever instinctively hating anyone before, but at that instant she hated Nathan Audley, not so much for his assassination of her character but for making her acknowledge an unfulfilled part of herself which she had thought she could ignore.

She of all people should have known that a person could survive without sex; it wasn't important. She had convinced David of this eventually and had never given him cause to doubt her honesty. Love had been enough and David had been her love.

If only he were here now, she thought, her grief resurrected with painful intensity from its dormant state. Nathan Audley wouldn't have dared touch her then.

CHAPTER TWO

IT WAS an hour before Matthew interrupted her painful
dissection of the preceding events. She glanced swiftly
at her reflection in the mirror before replying and saw
a calm, composed face looking back. She was still
surprised at how well she could mask any inner turmoil,
but as always she was grateful for the fact.

Unconsciously smoothing her mass of unruly curls,
she called him in.

'Annie?' He eyed her almost warily, which hardly
surprised her when she recalled the scene he'd
witnessed.

'Has he gone?' she asked, wondering what Matthew
was thinking. What had her stepson made of the sordid
scene he had walked in on?

He nodded. 'What exactly went on?' he asked bluntly
as he sat beside her on the bed. The concern that shone
from his bespectacled eyes was almost her undoing; she
swallowed the solid lump of emotion that clogged her
throat.

'I don't think your boss likes me much.' Her hand
covered the larger one he'd rested on her arm.

'It rather looked as if he liked you *too* much.' He
turned her hand over, examining the palm, the short
neat nails, the elegant spread of tapering fingers.
'Which, knowing Nathan and how bloody controlled
and elusive he normally is. . .' The concern had grown
deeper when he raised his eyes.

She could have laughed. He thought it had been
spontaneous, an outlet of warmth. . . Weren't kisses
generally those things? she recalled, the thought tinged
with sad irony. To enlighten him would place him in an

invidious position. Nathan held Matthew's career in his hands; now was not the time for honesty.

'Just a whim on his part,' she said, twisting her fingers free and avoiding the shrewd eyes.

'Nathan isn't in the habit of indulging whims.'

Annie, recalling the devastating things that the brush of his lips had done to her, greeted this information with relief; not that she fooled herself—any response he had wrung from her had been cold-bloodedly elicited, a weird punishment for thwarting him. She shuddered to think what havoc a man like that could wreak on an innocent bystander's life; giving himself full rein, the man would be ruthlessly destructive in his public or private life.

She made an impatient sound in her throat; the worst thing she could do would be to rouse her stepson's chivalrous instincts. 'Frankly, Matthew, I find the subject a little embarrassing. Put it down to an outlet for pre-examination nerves on my part and——' she made an all-encompassing gesture '—the charm of my personality. In truth, Matthew, it was nothing.'

He stood up, unfolding his long, lanky limbs slowly, with none of the fluid grace that Nathan exhibited. Unbidden, the comparison sprang to mind. 'Nothing,' she emphasised firmly. She forced her fingers to unfurl, feeling the discomfort of the half-moons her nails had impressed in the soft flesh.

'I'm glad, Annie.' He pushed his glasses further up his nose, a favourite tactic when he was choosing his words carefully. 'I'm glad, Annie,' he repeated. 'It's about time you had a relationship, but Nathan. . . I like him; he's brilliant, expects miracles and usually produces them.' He cleared his throat. 'Women seem to be drawn.'

'How nice for him.' The sneer remained in her mind and her face was blandly interested. 'You don't want me to be drawn.'

'The fact is, Annie, you're twenty-three, a widow,

gorgeous beyond most men's wildest dreams but on the experience front. . .' He dismissed his embarrassed gesture of denial with a lop-sided grin. 'Sexually a sixteen-year-old is probably more clued up. I know that, you know that and probably Josh suspects it,' he said thoughtfully. 'But most people, including Nathan, don't,' he added bluntly. 'Their expectations might be. . .'

'If you tell him. . .anyone. . .' A sudden fear gripped her and her dove-grey eyes deepened almost to indigo as she spoke. 'You wouldn't tell anyone, would you?'

He looked angry. 'You think I would. . .?' She looked guiltily back at him, ashamed of her swift rush of irrational fear. 'He had no right.' The words burst forth and his knuckles whitened in their grip on the door-handle as his eyes swivelled back to her. 'Bloody eighteen.'

The virulence in his voice shocked her. 'I knew before. It wasn't as if he tricked me,' she protested.

'Knew? Knew? Annie, you were eighteen; you worshipped the man. He knew that and he exploited your youth and emotions in a way I still can't forgive him for.'

'I loved David,' she said huskily. 'The age thing was irrelevant. Isn't a woman supposed to worship her husband?' she added, with a weak attempt at flippancy.

The miracle to her had been that he'd loved *her*, wanted her for his wife. David—remote, benevolent but distant. She had turned like a sun-seeking flower in response to the warmth he'd lavished on her. It had been like some delicious fairy-tale. But, as in all fairy-tales, there had been a dark cloud on the horizon.

'He lapped it up: little Annie, malleable and waiting to be led. But little Annie wasn't so little—still shy but with a body like Aphrodite's and a brain soaking up the information fed it like an eager sponge.'

The bitterness made her recoil; it hadn't been that way, she wanted to protest, hating this distorted vision.

'I blame the picture on the flyleaf of all those bloody books.' He visibly tried to de-escalate the aggression that seethed in his voice. 'He looked so noble. In reality, Annie, my father cheated you of your youth, tried to use it to cushion himself against the stark inevitability.'

'I wanted to share the little time he had left.'

'Did he give you a choice?' He gave an ironic laugh. 'You were besotted.' Her naïveté could be infuriating, he thought, looking into the carefully composed face, trying to see beyond the mystery of the beautiful eyes. 'You deserved more,' he said simply. 'By the way, I accepted the invite tonight on your behalf. I was a little worried but as you appear to feel so neutral about Nathan...' The swift change of subject was casually introduced.

She looked into the innocent pale blue eyes, alarm in her own. 'What invitation?'

'Dinner at the Crown, no less. Nathan is staying there.'

'I have to revise,' she responded with careful calm, while she felt her adrenalin push her metabolism into overdrive.

'A break is what you need, Annie. You look tense enough to snap...brittle.'

'I want to do well; it's a fairly normal state for a student this time of the year.'

'Do well for Dad.'

'For me,' she retorted swiftly, alarmed and shocked by the aggression in his voice.

'Let's face it, barring an act of God you're a first-class honours.'

'You think so?'

'I think so,' he told her soothingly. 'A nice evening with two devastatingly handsome men...good food. It's just what you need. Wear something sexy.'

Sexy? Did anything she possessed fit that description? She would have called him back but, considering she'd played the incident in the drawing-room down until it had seemed insignificant, what reason could she present that wouldn't make him suspect that all was not as straightforward as it seemed?'

The kiss, motivated by malice, had broken all her carefully constructed barriers. She wasn't ready or equipped to deal with the jolt of undiluted sexual hunger that had swamped her.

She closed her eyes, able to recall with exact precision the coiled tension in the hard, male body that had briefly held her. The compulsion to surrender had been bewildering and exhilarating. The demands of her senses had, for a few short, terrible moments, completely submerged the articulate clarity of her mental processes. She had totally believed in her ability to subdue and redirect hormonal cravings simply because she willed it, and then a man who made no attempt to disguise his contempt had rubbished this concept.

What a bizarre situation to be in—to be a widow without even the most basic grasp of sexual interplay, and certainly no practical experience to boast of. David had never attempted to disguise the truth from her—at least, not after he'd confessed his feelings for her. She'd felt that she had nothing to lose and so much to gain, she recalled. Being totally inexperienced sexually was probably best, she had earnestly explained; the fact that the medication had made him at least temporarily impotent meant nothing to her compared with his professed love.

She had been intoxicated—this incredible, talented man had said that she was the most important person in the world to him. The creeping disease had been the only obstacle to their future happiness.

At first its effects had been minimal, unnoticeable almost unless one knew what signs to look for. She had been fiercely optimistic that together they could conquer it. It had been six months before grim reality had made her doubt her ability to alter the future simply by determination. It had been then that the remission had given way to an acute episode.

Overnight the vigorous man had become an invalid and there had been no place for her own fear, not if she was to help him. The abrupt role reversal had been difficult to come to terms with but she had put her feelings in deep freeze, knowing that later there would be time to feel the pain; then David had needed her.

Only the knowledge that she couldn't have a child had made her conscious of their unconsummated union. In the circumstances the unusual state of their marriage had seemed almost irrelevant.

Her inexperience had not seemed a drawback during the two years of her widowhood and none of the prowling wolves she had kept at bay had challenged her deep conviction that she wasn't a highly sexed person. Her studies had absorbed her; David had encouraged her even before his interest had become more personal. Matthew had not followed the path his father had chosen and, in a way, she had taken his place. This fact had always made her feel slightly uneasy.

There was irony in her dressing to dine with the man who had avowed his intention to evict her from her precious home. He couldn't, she reminded herself, but, recalling the inflexibility in those deep green eyes, she couldn't repress a shudder.

She was safe from the worst of his offensive behaviour, she told herself. Even so, she was unable to banish the incredible edginess. Matthew's right, I am brittle, she told herself. But the thought of enduring an evening of undiluted contempt filled her with dread.

The Tudor inn where Nathan was staying was set in several acres of parkland—an exclusive establishment she hadn't visited since David's death. The food was, she knew, excellent, but her usual appetite had vanished. Her stomach was knotted with nervous tension, but none of this showed on her face or in her movements.

Above average height, her figure, slenderly statuesque, drew curious glances as she and Matthew entered the restaurant. The simplicity of the plain black gown she wore emphasised the curves of her slim, firm body. Her pale complexion glowed against the sombre colour and her hair lay in a fiery nimbus around her delicately moulded face. The candles set in sconces caught threads of molten fire running through the burnished mass as she was led to the table.

She felt an emotion hard to define as pleasurable or painful; it corkscrewed through her as her eyes met the green eyes shot with tigerish amber glints. Hopefully she waited for the breathless feeling to dissipate; why should the anticipation of this dreadful evening open the door to this ambiguous exhilaration?

The tight smile didn't reach her eyes as Nathan rose. A loose-fitting Armani suit and a cream silk shirt buttoned up to the neck, minus a tie, reinforced his exclusive image and did nothing to disguise the power of his broad-shouldered, athletic frame. His eyes skimmed over her, not missing any detail and no doubt, she decided, sourly placing a price tag on her inexpensive wardrobe out of sheer force of habit.

She was glad of the interruption when the proprietor descended upon her. 'We have missed you, Mrs Selby. It's delightful to see you again.'

Annie's smile was warm for a moment; the caution that governed her features dissolved, allowing the full luminosity of her beauty to shine through. 'Poor students can't afford your outrageous prices,' she replied lightly.

'The professor is much missed.'

'Yes, he is,' she said gravely. The genuineness of his expression touched her on the raw and she felt ashamed of the stab of irritation. Without her brilliant husband she was, as always, something of an oddity—the window-dressing without a window. The cynical thought shocked her and an expression of confusion flitted across her face.

The two men spoke at length about business matters and she sipped a soft drink. She allowed her mind to drift, dwelling on her growing resentment of the way this man's presence could reduce her serenity to anarchic chaos; the desire to be out of his presence and gone was incredibly strong.

This is just a business dinner, she reminded herself, angry at her over-reaction. She'd probably be called on to do nothing more than pick up a glass with a steady hand and smile at appropriate moments; if this was anything to go by they might even forget she was there.

'You appear to be well-known here.' The laser regard turned without warning.

She slopped some liquid on to her lap and felt ridiculously flustered. 'David entertained here sometimes,' she agreed, finding her poise after a brief, internal battle. How did the man manage to import so much innuendo into an innocent statement? Perhaps he was worried that she'd proposition the waiter; if she had been convinced that she could carry it off, it might almost have been worth it to see his face.

A dark brow raised. 'I'd have thought that with a house like Chausey. . .'

'Annie is an appalling cook,' Matthew supplied, with an affectionate grin.

She accepted the insult with a cheerful smile. 'Basic' would have been more accurate, but she tolerated teasing on her culinary skills with good humour.

'No live-in cook?'

'My aunt was the cook; after she died David didn't replace her.'

'A regular upstairs-downstairs romance,' he drawled, his tone amused, the glint in his eyes less benevolent. 'She never got to see you as lady of the manor. I'm sure she would have been proud of how far you've gone.'

In other words, I've been groomed for the task! she thought furiously, not fooled by the bland expression. The implied criticism of her beloved aunt which her sensitive ear detected made her grow rigid with temper. She was proud of her aunt, of her roots. The elderly woman had taken her in as a toddler when she had been far from young herself, after Annie's parents had died tragically in a car crash. Meeting his hard green gaze with scorn, she wondered whether to add snobbishness to all his other unpleasant traits.

'Not far really, just half a mile up the driveway.'

'I wasn't actually thinking geographically.'

At that point a waiter, apologising for the interruption, announced that there was an urgent call for Mr Selby. Matthew, who had been observing the undercurrent of tension at the table with mixed feelings, excused himself.

'Alone at last,' Nathan murmured as she toyed with her fish.

'Not for long, hopefully,' she replied drily. Concealing her hostility seemed a waste of energy. 'I'm puzzled as to why I merited an invitation at all. Doesn't Matthew's presence limit the degree to which you can insult me?'

'But Matthew isn't here,' he pointed out.

She raised her eyes from the plate, her expression cultivated to be provocative and taunting. 'A temporary situation.'

The green eyes smouldered as they homed in on her playfully pursed lips. He didn't even have the decency to be furtive, she thought, trying to hang on to her studied casualness, which was hard, when the said eyes narrowed in speculation as he permitted himself the slightest, most violent smile she had ever seen.

'I think you'll find Matthew's presence is urgently

required elsewhere.' His teeth flashed once more, very white against the Mediterranean tan.

Annie blinked, stunned as the significance of this statement sank in. Such barefaced manipulation was too outrageous to contemplate. 'You seem to have gone to elaborate lengths.'

She hoped he'd be disappointed by her lack of reaction. There was nothing to read in his lazy-eyed scrutiny—lazy only like a cat waiting to pounce on its prey, she decided, pictorially sketching in her own features on the victim. No way was she going to let him provide the hoops for her to jump through.

'For the pleasure of your company.'

'I'm flattered beyond measure,' she countered drily. A convulsive shiver rippled down the length of her spine as he inclined his head a little closer, the movement diminishing the distance between them.

His compelling eyes seemed to be seeking a clue to what lay beneath her calm exterior. He had the aura of someone quite capable of reading minds. . .

She dismissed this whimsical idea, deriding herself for being so vulnerable to his predatory air of command. He probably practises looking dangerous in the mirror, she told herself, trying to squirm free of the oppressive spell she felt he was weaving about her.

'Sorry, you two, but my presence is required in Reading. A case of bureaucracy gone crazy. Unless you want to take charge, boss?'

'Delegation, Matt, is the key to my success.' He slanted Annie a taunting look as she gritted her teeth. As much as she longed to fling her knowledge of his blatant manipulation into the pot, and to hell with the consequences, she knew she could not, for Matthew's sake.

'I thought you had things pretty well sorted there, Matt,' he was saying, his tone bordering on the censorious, and Matthew was looking apologetic and worried.

He dropped a distracted kiss on Annie's cheek, his thoughts clearly dwelling on his problem. 'I'll need the car, Annie.'

'I'll see the lady safely home.'

Annie, awake to every nuance, heard the inflexion he placed on 'lady'. She threw him a look of hostile loathing. 'I'm quite capable of getting home.' She would sooner walk than share a care with Nathan. 'Don't worry, love.' Her fingers trailed along Matthew's jacket sleeve, reluctant to break contact. She had a ridiculous impulse to beg him not to go.

I can deal with Nathan Audley, she told herself sternly, quashing the premonitory feelings that sliced through all logic. 'You must be too tired to drive,' she said, knowing she was clutching at straws and furious because the fact was affording Nathan malicious amusement.

Matthew flicked her chin affectionately. 'This fragile frame,' he told her, 'conceals an iron constitution.' He turned to exchange a few words on technical details with his boss before leaving.

'Such concern—very maternal.'

Annie maintained her silence as he nodded dismissively at the sweet trolley and she did likewise. For once her sweet tooth had deserted her. 'We don't have a mother-son relationship,' she replied as the trolley trundled away.

'I can imagine.'

Smug, supercilious... Every time he opened his mouth and sneered at her with that austere superiority she wanted to disfigure his patrician face. The strength of her anger was so intense, so primitive that the fact that she was experiencing it made her feel disorientated.

'Feel free to let your imagination run riot. I can imagine what an impoverished personal life you must lead; living vicariously is so sad, I always feel.' A spasm of fastidious distaste passed over her face and his head reared as though she'd suddenly been granted his complete attention.

'I feel I should point out that no pressure you subject me to will alter my decision not to move out to Chausey,' she went on. 'In fact, the fact that you want it provides me with adequate incentive not to.'

She shook her head back and rested her chin on her steepled fingers; her smile was sweetly malicious and she gave a sigh of satisfaction. That had felt *good*.

Nathan's eyes slid from the flame-bright hair, as it fell back from her face and resettled itself into a flaming mass down her back, to her bosom, heaving dramatically with emotion.

Her eyes flashed. While she never chose to flaunt her body she was damned if he'd make her feel self-conscious. She had no intention of being subjected to his prurient perusal any longer.

'That statement is surprising, considering your touching concern for Matt's welfare.'

Annie, who had been gathering herself for a sweeping exit, paused. 'What circumstances?'

'I thought you and he were so close. Hasn't he told you?'

The taunt, the challenge that glittered in his eyes brought a silent snarl to her throat. In the past she'd endured it when acquaintances *en masse* had assumed the worst of her motives. Yet here she was consumed by a simmering rage. What was this man's opinion? Nothing. Mentally she snapped her fingers. When he approved of her then was the time to worry, she told herself. One day she'd disabuse him of his misconceptions and watch his face... So much for the infallible Nathan Audley.

'Told me what?' she said flatly. So he was writing the dialogue, stringing her along; she had to ask anyway and he knew it.

'Matt's had an offer of a partnership...in the Bahamas—a resort hotel.'

She felt a surge of delight; she had been expecting something dire, not something like this. 'It's marvellous, just what he's always wanted,' she burst out impetuously, her eyes shining with genuine pleasure. Then a sudden frown drew her dark eyebrows into a straight line. He hadn't said a word. Why?

'All he needs is the finance.'

He watched, unblinking, as sudden realisation crept like a cloud across her eyes. He frowned as if the transparency of her reaction spoilt the balance of some mental equation.

'Chausey?' Her voice was nothing more than a sigh.

'With a sitting tenant, that isn't on, is it, darling?' he drawled.

Her eyes opened wide with protest. 'Matthew loves Chausey,' she protested, shaking her head. 'His family have lived there for generations; years back they owned all the land around. *You* see a pile of bricks and stone. What would you know about the heart of a home?' she sneered. He was suggesting sacrilege. Matthew loved Chausey; it was his home.

'Used to, honey. . .' he replied, unmoved by her apparent distress. 'I find it quaint the way you fling around words like "heart" and "home" when we both know that both terms are alien concepts to you, sweetheart. Matt doesn't give——' he snapped his long, lean fingers, the sound like a rifle-shot '—*that* for the house; his vision is focused on the future.'

'What would you know about it?'

The angular jaw tightened and his lips thinned. 'Whose roots are we talking about here, sweetheart? I don't see any blue blood circulating in your sweetly opportunist veins. It may surprise you that I was brought up in a house not dissimilar to Chausey.'

'Then go back to it,' she spat, knowing and hating the petulance in her voice.

'That isn't possible,' he replied bleakly. The green eyes were charged with animosity as they homed in on her with an intensity that was impossible to tear her attention from.

'It'll always be there for Matt, that gnawing knowledge that he had his dream within his grasp. It's enough to make the most well-balanced soul brood,' he mused. Eventually he'll start allocating blame. Right now the pleasure of your smile is balm enough to make you his favourite stepmother. Later. . .' he sucked in his breath and shrugged. . . 'he'll resent you for being the obstacle.

'But by then I expect you'll have moved on, so what the hell?' he sneered. 'You're a bright girl who's no doubt already caught on to the fact that your appeal is transitory. Best choose the dying ones—no time for the disillusion to settle in.

'If I were generous I'd say that a grasping little social parasite like you doesn't possess any honest emotion and so can't be totally blamed for destroying her stepping-stones.' The green eyes shone with gleaming contempt and he replaced his glass on the table with a loud thud. 'I don't feel generously inclined when it comes to women like you,' he rasped.

'Two years with some men would be worth more than a lifetime with others, and as for a cynical, vindictive bastard like you I'd prefer a life sentence with the devil.'

He'd touched, without knowing it, on a raw spot. It had always plagued her. Would David have married her if he hadn't known he was dying—known it if not acknowledged it? 'The only commodity you deal in is cynicism. I hardly expect a man like you to understand the concept of love.'

The laugh was like shards of glass, abrasive and discordant. 'Love is the fiction the general populace swallows to maintain the status quo.' He intertwined his long brown fingers and regarded her with indolent distaste. 'I've no doubt that, overcome by your great love, you reserved enough energy to squeeze what you could from the elder Selby. Don't you think it's time

you gave the son a break? It's no secret that David was
comfortably off; now the money's magically gone. I
wonder where?'

She felt outrage vibrate through her body. She had
squandered David's fortune, had she? If only he knew.
The passionate desire to cling to life had been strong
in her husband; the diets, medications and all manner
of alternative treatments had been begun with hope
and discarded with gloom.

The last and financially incapacitating avenue they
had explored had sent them to a Mexican clinic boast-
ing a radical new treatment. Unlike the other treatments, which had at least given hope, this had been so
punitive in nature that she, after much soul-searching,
had persuaded him to discontinue. The psychological
drain had been even greater than the financial one and
David had never really continued his fight after that.

'A girl must protect her future,' she said, her eyes
glittering with feverish intensity. 'You did point out
that my charms are bound to fade.'

'If I pay you off?' The disgust in his austere face
gave her great satisfaction.

'Are you extremely rich, then?' she enquired sweetly.
Why not fulfil his expectations? she decided recklessly.

'Extremely,' he agreed, his nostrils flaring as he
regarded her with acute disgust tempered, she thought,
with some complacency at having his opinion
vindicated.

He seemed to gain some perverse pleasure in considering her a tramp. . .a self-seeking little gold-digger,
so smugly contemptuous and certain of her market
value. 'But what's in it for you?' she enquired with an
air of bewilderment.

'Is that relevant?' The chocolatey, gravelly purr was
clipped and impatient. A thick, dark lock of hair fell on
to his forehead, to be impatiently brushed back.

The hair at least refused to conform to his uniform
perfection. It was thick, inclined to wave, and although

well cut had no neatly blow-dried appearance. Annie felt herself mentally experimenting with the tactile sensation of pushing her fingers deep into the luxuriant dark growth to feel the outline of his skull.

Eyes blank, she stared at her fingertips, which tingled, and sucked her breath in in a noisy gasp as she realised what she had been contemplating. She saw his brows rise as a flush of tell-tale colour seeped into her face. 'Humour me,' she suggested, her aberration making her prickle with high-voltage antagonism.

'I'd hate to see Matt's career blighted by an avaricious bitch like you.'

Something behind his eyes combined with the rigidity in his habitually languid poise made her heightened senses take a quantum leap in comprehension. A woman had actually pulled a fast one on Nathan Audley. She felt like applauding.

'Matthew is what you once were; how quaint, and noble too, of you to feel the urge to smooth his path.' He had underestimated her perception and she saw it momentarily in his eyes. Then the instant readjustment took place and the shutters were back in place. 'I'm amazed you don't just finance him yourself, or doesn't your affinity extend that far?'

'Matthew doesn't need a patron, just a chance to prove his worth.'

He'd hit where it hurt but he didn't know it. She was so shallow in his book that she wouldn't even know how to consider anyone else's interests. If what he had been saying was true... She couldn't think about it now; she just had to get away from this abhorrent man.

'How much?' she asked crudely. The sum he mentioned only served to increase her sense of outrage. He smiled with grim contempt, misinterpreting her inarticulate gasp.

'I thought I was to be punished, not rewarded,' she reminded him hoarsely.

'Time punishes women like you,' he said with casual

scorn, the movement of his shapely, elegant hands dismissive. He flicked up his cuff and deliberately looked at his watch. 'Expedience on this occasion seemed appropriate.'

'Such constraint,' she said slowly, 'does you justice. However——' she tilted her chin to a defiant angle and looked at him, her eyes luminous with proud contempt '—my price will always be too high for you. I find you have the worst brand of arrogance I have yet encountered. Intellectual snobbery, middle-class insularity—I thought I'd seen it all.' She was passionately glad to see him freeze in surprise. 'You, however, are in a class of your own. I am not for sale at any price.' She rose then, tall, slender and trembling with righteous indignation.

Explosive anger released, she felt nauseous in reaction and the dull headache that had been brewing swung into throbbing life. She couldn't afford to display weakness before this barbaric man. He had none of the finer, gentler feelings that she so greatly admired in men; he was brutish and ruthless. He wasn't a man to stand being thwarted, she knew; this had been a novel experience for him, she suspected. His single-minded ambition might have been wrapped in a package that could be urbane and charming but she for one wasn't fooled.

'How do you intend to get home?'

'I would imagine it's not beyond my capabilities to get a taxi,' she replied sarcastically. The prickle down her spine had forewarned her that he had followed her into the foyer. People had stared at them but she had been too overwrought to notice and he had a genuine indifference to being the cynosure of all eyes.

The fingers on her arm wouldn't accept her refusal to face him. Not wanting an undignified tussle, she removed her eyes from the empty reception desk.

'You're h-h——' Her throat closed suddenly. He radiated a vigour so masculine, so tangible that it hit her almost like a physical blow. As if under a warm sun

that melted away inhibitions she felt his smouldering
eyes strip away the protective layers intricately woven
around her.

No wonder she had felt antagonistic when faced with
such undiluted magnetic masculinity; it had been a
basic, protective instinct. It had been too dangerous to
recognise the earthy magnetism because in doing so
she had to recognise her own vulnerability to it.

His eyes gripped her—green eyes, regressed to some
primitive level that was unfamiliar, but how that stare
made her ache with frustration that she couldn't begin
to understand. She took a deep, soothing draught of
oxygen to replenish her starving lungs.

Don't fall apart, Annie, she told herself, letting her
head loll forward and the blood feed her brain. I'm
sure he has this effect on all females from nine to
ninety; it's irrelevant. She felt slightly better but the
sudden, painful acknowledgement lingered in her
senses like a pungent, evocative odour.

'You're hurting me.' Her voice was throaty and as
she inclined her chin her slender throat seemed vulnerable; the skin had a look of marble against the stark
black of her gown. Her skin wasn't cold, though; she
felt hot despite the shudder that rippled through her.

The green eyes that held hers grew sardonic; with a
small, tight smile he removed his hands from her arm.
She repressed a slightly hysterical laugh as she inferred
from his ostentatious movement that he imagined that
she had found his physical contact distasteful. So she
did, but not exactly in the way she felt she ought to.
Damn the man, she thought. Then, in a businesslike
manner, she asked the young man who had just
appeared at the reception desk for a taxi.

CHAPTER THREE

'FOG, what fog?'

The young man sitting behind the reception desk looked nonplussed by this dismissive approach to his politely expressed information.

'Visibility is poor in this immediate area and none of the local firms are accepting fares at the moment,' he reiterated apologetically.

'There was no fog an hour ago,' Annie said, as though arguing the point could alter the facts of the situation, despite the sinking feeling in the pit of her stomach that told her otherwise. 'Matthew left half an hour ago.'

'Fog can be abrupt and I believe the weather forecast did mention that there was a possibility,' Nathan offered. The young man looked grateful and she ground her teeth.

'Why don't you slither off somewhere suitably reptilian?' she snapped. She could do without his patronising scrunity at the moment.

As she glared at him she saw the subtle shift in his features, the flicker of expression in his eyes, and read, to her chagrin, amusement. 'No doubt this rounds off the evening nicely from your point of view,' she accused. 'You insult me, treat me like a piece of merchandise to be eliminated, send Matthew out on some wild-goose chase. . .and he'll probably end up in some pile-up on the motorway. Fog!'

'I have no control over the elements,' he observed mildly, appearing to grow more economical with emotion the more heated and near to losing control she became.

'I'm sure you'd remedy that if the opportunity arose.'

'Oh, I don't know. I think the unpredictability of British weather adds a certain piquancy to life.'

She felt the victim of a cascade of violent emotions.

A starvation victim suddenly faced with a banquet could not have felt more confused or numbed. 'You can drive me,' she announced suddenly, when the gimlet gaze was too much to endure.

He shook his head, the satirical lift of one brow seemed to her eyes distinctly satanic. 'That would be unwise. I'd hate to be responsible for breaking that beautiful neck.'

Her breathing became distinctly laboured as his eyes moved down her white throat at a leisurely pace. 'Wouldn't that be a solution to your problem?' she said hoarsely.

'I could never deliberately mar a work of art,' he said tersely. For a split-second, while she was holding her breath and wondering how to respond, his eyes touched hers briefly but intimately in a way she had never encountered before. The flare that dilated his pupils conveyed such ferocity, such ambivalent hunger and distaste that she took several seconds to recover while he was speaking to the young man, who was giving a convincing performance of being oblivious to the content of their conversation.

Such delightful manners, she thought wryly; so like my own usually. Since the moment she'd laid eyes on this man her behaviour patterns had become completely aberrant. Where, she wondered, was cool, serene, well-balanced Annie? The Annie who never let her emotions surface to embarrass people?

It had been like that when David died. She had moved through the subsequent events as if she were working her way through some film script—outwardly calm, inwardly falling to pieces. Until it had happened she had never quite believed that there would be no reprieve.

'There are no rooms.'

The words pulled her free from her reverie. 'I don't want a room. I want to go *home*.' The last word came out with such force and was packed with so much longing that she wildly summoned up some statement to lessen the impact. 'I'll walk.'

'Five miles?'

'Not far.'

'Along lanes with nil visibility—in those.' His nod indicated the soft leather pumps with the slender heel that she was wearing.

Annie's jaw tightened. He just loved pointing out the obvious, especially when it made her look stupid. 'I don't have much choice, do I?'

'I have a suite.'

'In keeping with your station in life.'

He inhaled deeply, his eyes narrowing. 'Naturally,' he agreed drily, his expression somehow making her feel spiteful and childish. 'As I was saying, I have an empty room which you can feel at liberty to make use of. As it is, I feel your slightly hysterical presence in the lobby is becoming an embarrassment.'

'I'll wait until the fog lifts, or hitch,' she added.

'That would be a bright move. Am I to assume that you find me more potentially hazardous than the sort of person who'd offer a woman alone, dressed like you, a lift?' She felt strangely defenceless under the hard, unamused scrutiny of his thickly fringed eyes.

'The owner knows me; I'm sure he can arrange something,' she said loftily.

'I had already thought of that. Believe you me, getting you off my hands was my first choice. Your friend——' he managed to imply all sorts of unpleasant things in his voice, and a prickle of cold anger travelled the length of her rigid spine '—has gone home already, to a wife who is imminently expecting to present him with child. The staff here cannot throw anyone out to accommodate you; so face it, honey, you're left with me. Keep a vigil at the window if you must and call a taxi the instant the fog lifts, but stop behaving like a prima donna,' he advised tersely.

The censure made her flush. 'I've had a trying day.'

'Had a cosy afternoon planned with—what was he called?—Jack, did you? My condolences. . .'

'Josh,' she replied swiftly. 'Josh has to work and so do I.'

'He's a student too, is he?'

'You make it sound unsavoury. Actually,' she corrected him, 'he's a fellow.' His derisive expression confirmed the scorn she'd detected in his voice. 'Do I detect a certain antagonism for academia? Didn't you go to university?'

'I was too busy building a business.'

'A self-made man, no less. How impressive,' she drawled, happy to see a faint flush of anger beneath his tan. 'But you do yourself an injustice; surely yours is an empire?' She was the first to drop her gaze as he levelled a hard, brooding scrutiny at her face, no longer so sure that she was happy to have annoyed him. It was a bit like baiting an unpredictable but lethal wild animal—not the sort of sport sensible women like herself went in for.

Eyes half hooded, the plane of his high cheekbones adding to the shadow along his jawline, he muttered under his breath, 'This woman is ridiculous. I refuse to exchange childish insults with a female clearly used to being indulged by every man she deigns to smile at. If you want to theorise about my prejudices we can at least do so in relative privacy.'

She was a tall woman but his size made her feel overpowered as he propelled her before him up the stairs as if her acquiescence was a foregone conclusion.

The Crown had few rooms but those it did have were lavishly and richly appointed—quaint and beamed enough to appeal to the tourist, and romantic enough for a honeymoon, with the obligatory four-poster bed in each room.

She stood staring at the bed, for some reason unable to tear her eyes away from the elaborate decorated canopy with its delicate crewel work. When she did avert her eyes she saw that her host was opening a laptop computer which he'd set up on an oak desk. The fact that he was ignoring her unaccountably piqued her.

'My room?'

His eyes flicked from the screen which had just sprung to life. 'I have work to do.'

'So have I, but I don't expect you to lose any sleep over the fact.'

'Don't the studies interfere with your social life?'

Annie expelled an explosive breath but she summoned a sweet, taunting smile. 'I lead a full and varied life and try not to neglect any area. With luck I probably won't have to sleep with too many of the faculty to get a decent degree.'

'I never doubted your intellect, Annie, just your motivation. It's your brains that make you so dangerous.'

Her eyes darkened. Motivation—she could tell him a thing or two about that. 'My husband believed in me. If it hadn't been for him, after my aunt died I'd have left school and got some dead-end job; but he——' Her voice, deep and intense, cracked, and when she continued the pain of her loss was in her voice. 'I have every intention of being what he wanted.'

His control was so supreme that not by so much as a flicker did Nathan betray the surprise he felt at the blast of passion in her face as she spoke of her dead husband. It sparked a vibrancy, a luminosity that transcended the undoubted beauty she possessed. 'Is it entirely healthy to be motivated by a desire to please the dead?' He sounded coldly speculative.

She wanted to hit him then so badly that she didn't trust herself to move.

'I mean, when you've done what he wanted what

then? Do you hold a seance before you make your next career move?'

'I'm doing what I want.' The man had no scruples, no humanity; he attacked with whatever weapon he discovered hurt most. She was trembling. David's death had happened two years ago and she was resilient. It was just his derisive attitude that was painful.

Most people she mixed with knew of, if they hadn't known, David, and his memory was revered in the university, his worth and his opinions never questioned. First Matthew and now this man—at least Matthew had the right; it angered her, hearing Nathan Audley being so openly contemptuous.

'Not getting what you want—that's all that bothers you. You sneer at my morals but men like you are motivated solely by avarice, the desire to accumulate wealth and the power that goes along with it.

'You want Chausey and I don't believe for one instant that a man like you——' her nostrils dilated in distaste and her eyes iced over '—cares a jot for Matthew's future. That's just a convenient device to disguise the unacceptability of your motives. I won't see Chausey become some anonymous hotel. Maybe you made moral distinctions once——'

She broke off, her voice beginning to degenerate into a tremulous whisper. She made a gesture of rejection with her hands, the controlled movement more eloquent than words. She rejected everything this man stood for. Tenderness and compassion were beyond him; he was all tempered steel, ruthlessness, charisma—so much so that he probably made the unacceptable fact of finance seem attractive.

The fact was that even she could feel confused when exposed to the menace of predatory sensuality, and she had never been impressed by power and wealth—she appreciated less flamboyant qualities. While she recognised her unexpected weakness in responding and despised it, she knew it was just a superficial response to his aura of earthy sensuality.

Nathan crossed his legs at the ankle and her eyes reluctantly flickered to the muscular strength of his long legs. The pressure of his heel against the deep Aubusson carpet twisted the seat around. He seemed unnaturally relaxed considering the insults she'd just thrown at him; a couple of casual flicks and the computer screen went black.

'Is it my wealth you object to, Annie, or me?' he mused, half to himself, the long fingers steepled together as he shot her a look from half-closed, lazy eyelids. 'Are you trying to tell me that it was love that made you marry a man who had the financial security most people would envy? A man who had made it to the top in a world which gave him a good deal of clout, not to mention status. Was it the subtle intellect of this man that had you so hot or were you as influenced by the things he represented, the things he had to offer?

'I'd say the academic world can rival even politics when it comes to dirty tricks. The naïve professor is a thing of the past. I find it hard to believe you were married to such a flawless saint.'

She listened to the soft words which somehow increased the anxiety she felt threefold. Suddenly she was reminded of Matthew's bitter accusations earlier.

'Money is a commodity with little inherent value to me. It gives me freedom to live life as near to my own terms as possible and, as clichéd as it sounds, I do provide a few people with a means of supporting themselves. I like to call the shots but it means I take the falls; the ultimate responsibility is mine and I like it that way. I can take the isolation.'

'Unlike lesser mortals,' she sneered, his brand of unapologetic arrogance making her want to withdraw, not wanting to hear any further revelations. It surprised her how forthright he could be; she hadn't expected this opening up—it was confusing.

He spun the chair slightly on its axis and thrust his hands into his pockets. 'If you like,' he agreed, with no touch of complacency. 'I deal with ruthless people, so, to survive, I have to be able to deal on equal terms. The distinction between private life and public blurred some time ago.'

The smile—ironic, not quite reaching the green eyes—flashed forth. 'That's part of the reason why marriage, for me, would be doomed to failure. I could never abandon my defences sufficiently.

'As for Matt—I like the boy; he has potential, and it came as something of a surprise to me to learn that I was willing to exert myself, just a little, to smooth his path. He's refreshingly uncomplicated.'

That was something she could never accuse this man of being. As for this apparent openness, was it some further trick to throw her off guard? She rubbed the furrow between her eyebrows at the point where the headache was sending darts of pain to the area behind her eye sockets. 'If that goes any way towards making him like you I'll put any obstacle I can in the way.'

Even as she spoke she knew there was no possibility of this; he was impregnable, this man—a brilliant predator not cast in the same mould as Matthew. She sighed, unaware that the pain she was experiencing—at least the physical pain of a blinding headache—was clearly displayed in the taut lines of strain around her eyes and the vagueness in them.

It was so difficult to concentrate and her thoughts had brought the earlier accusations he'd made into play. Did Matthew truly need the money the sale of Chausey could provide? Was she the only obstacle? She caught her lower lip between her teeth—a full lip, indicative of a passionate, stubborn nature.

'Did you care more for the house or the man?' His sardonic expression intensified as she made a small, outraged gasp.

'I thought you'd decided I cared about no one but myself.'

'I'm prepared to concede you're a little more complex than I had anticipated.'

The sensation of unreality increased as she encountered the ruthless surveillance of the gleaming green stare. That's big of him, she thought. 'I fail to see what possible interest the constituents of my personality could be to you.'

His laughter was arid, empty of humour. 'Now naïveté would be pushing the bounds of credulity.'

What was the man talking about now? She wished she could shake free from the painful intrusions that were imploding with consistent cruelty in her skull. Migraine. At home she had medication that could halt its progress, but she wasn't at home. 'You haven't flinched from calling a spade a bloody shovel up to this point, Mr Audley, so why not spell it out for me?'

'I was suggesting that we postpone our wrangling and explore further possibilities.' A frown flickered in his eyes at her blank stare of frustrated incomprehension. 'You can hardly deny the fact that you've been dramatically receptive to me as a man from the moment we met. I can see you're going to deny just that,' he said a moment later, with a degree of weary resignation.

'Look, I concede you were obviously not motivated by purely materialistic reasoning when you married. I'm even prepared to take it as read that you were faithful after a fashion while the marriage lasted.'

Annie's perception suddenly sharpened. He was propositioning her—in an irritated, jaded fashion, true, but, none the less, that was where he was going. 'But now I'm fair game. The frustrated widow.'

'Hardly frustrated.' His lip curled.

'I'd never be that frustrated,' she assured him, anticipating the insult. 'Besides, I thought you were the financier monk,' she sneered provocatively. 'Wed to your refined art of accumulating wealth.'

He rose from the chair in one fluid motion and it took all her self-control not to retreat to the other side of the room. 'I said marriage was not on my agenda, not that I had taken a vow of celibacy. You can hardly expect me to believe I'm too old for you.'

'I'm sure you've got an enviable libido but I'm prepared to take it on trust. Displays are quite unnecessary,' she said with dismissive irony. She concentrated on the anger she felt at the cold-blooded invitation to sex; she was far too discriminating ever to have contemplated a casual affair. He imagined that she was the product of some Lolita-like adolescence, she reminded herself.

The headache had progressed and now her vision was subjected to violent shifts as though the room, if not spinning on its axis, was certainly shifting. The next stage was. . .ugh! What was she going to do now? she wondered despairingly.

Nathan's jaw was tight, his expression darkly insolent, and Annie could see that he wasn't going to let the matter rest. 'Where the hell are you going?' His voice followed her as she fled the room.

The bathroom was, thankfully, close at hand. Her needs had been too urgent to contemplate items such as doors, and the sight of a pair of gleaming, hand-tooled leather shoes on the tiled floor beside her made her groan afresh. The indignity of having her illness witnessed was terrible. David had hated any sign of physical weakness—that was partly why he'd found his own to difficult to come to terms with.

'I have a migraine.' She was still on her knees but managed to drag herself upright, grabbing hold of the vanity unit. The effort was exhausting and her balance was less than perfect, so she was grateful for the water that he sent rushing into the basin. She dabbed at her face and rinsed her mouth from the water beaker he placed in her trembling hand.

'Why didn't you say something?'

'What for?' she said dispiritedly. She didn't have the energy to protest when, with a fluent curse, he scooped her up into his arms. She was too immersed in the painful throbbing in her skull and the dizzying nausea to register more than the elusive masculine scent of the man and the impression of awesome strength that filtered into her brain.

Five minutes later she was lying on the bed, the overhead lights having been extinguished. Her dress had been removed with an expertise that any other time would have made her indignant, but right now she only felt gratitude.

She didn't open her eyes when the cool sponge soaked up the sheen of sweat that had broken out over her body; it was blissfully soothing.

'Shall I call your doctor?'

'It won't last too much longer. I'll be out of the way soon.' He must be cursing her, she realised. The last thing he had wanted was an invalid on his hands.

Painfully she made her eyelids operate; the subdued light sent lights dancing across her vision. Her distorted brain played her false because for an instant, before she closed her eyes, she imagined that a fleeting compassion softened the gem-like hardness in his eyes. That was ridiculous and possibly wishful thinking; his actions had been practical, she told herself. Just because he wasn't thrown by illness it didn't mean he didn't object to being subjected to her fragility.

'I want to sleep.'

The silence continued, dark and comforting, and the feathery touch across her forehead was part of the dream.

'Tea, hot and sweet.'

'M-Matthew,' she stammered, looking around a completely unfamiliar bedroom. Then it came back—her humiliating reduction to invalid. 'Where is. . .?' She looked around furtively as though the owner of the room was about to materialise.

'Nathan had an early appointment in Edinburgh. He called me and told me to hotfoot it back. Actually, I don't know what the idiots were panicking about; I wasn't actually needed. Poor Annie!' He smiled in sympathy, used to her spasmodic headaches. 'Been keeping off the chocolate, have you? It was good of Nathan to let you stay here; I bet it threw him.' He shuddered, recalling the violence of her attacks.

'Actually, he coped pretty well,' she said in a distant voice. With some amazement she was sifting through the evidence that led her to this conclusion. Suddenly her eyes slid to her body, its outline masked by the light covering. She reached for and gulped her tea; her mouth felt dry and stale. 'Give me five minutes, Matthew, and I'll be ready,' she said decisively, a firm smile accompanying the words.

After a speculative glance at her still pale face, he acquiesced. She threw back the bedclothes and gave a groan of dismay. The strapless black bra and silky pants were all she was wearing. The muscles of her stomach quivered as she realised who had removed her outer layers.

Her eyes tried to see herself as he had—creamy skin with a faint, pearly lustre, long legs, the dip of her hips feminine but not lushly so, the curve of the thigh almost boyish, flat, taut belly, high ribcage and full breasts, barely confined by the silky binding.

Suddenly she needed to cover herself, wanting to banish the incident. . .the man from her mind. She knew that the latter at least wasn't realistic. Nathan wasn't a man to disappear before he was ready, and then he would do it with profound efficiency.

Did he discard all his women without regret? she

wondered. Or had there been one...? This line of speculation was ridiculous, she told herself.

Ignoring the pull of the bath, she just washed her hands and face and slid the black dress over her head. Rolling the lace-topped stay-up stockings over her calves, she had a sudden, vivid image of lean brown fingers, elegantly precise, brushing against her skin to remove the same items. A sensation strange and uncomfortable flowered in the pit of her belly, sending a fluid heat through her lower limbs.

She shook her head and cursed as her nail snagged the fine fabric. Wretched man! The worst part was that, no matter how loathsome he had been initially, yesterday, once she had been in need of help and painfully vulnerable, he had done everything required of him with clinical efficiency. Perversely she knew she'd have felt easier if he'd continued to be abusive or at least been repelled—throwing up wasn't exactly aesthetically pleasing.

Annie remained silent, through her mind was busy, on the journey back to Chausey. 'I've been thinking, Matthew.' The grunt encouraged her to continue. 'Would you mind awfully if I moved into the gate-house? I mean, it's such an enormous house with only me in it and it costs a fortune to heat.' She held her breath.

'Annie, I can help out more financially; I knew you were stretching yourself too thin.' His face settled into rueful anger as he drove cautiously along the narrow lane. 'If only Dad hadn't persisted in falling for every charlatan out to make a quick buck.'

'He never lost hope.'

'Just a hell of a lot of money.'

'In fact, Matthew, I'm nervous all alone.'

'Nervous...you?' he said incredulously, glancing into the steadfast clarity of her gaze. 'Since when?'

'The old house has too many memories.'

'I should have realised. . .but, Annie, you love the place.'

I do, I do, she wanted to shout; she loved every mellow stone, every inconvenient nook and cranny. 'It's only a place,' she said, with a shrug. Much, much more, a voice screamed in her head. 'After all, you've lived there longer than I. . .your family.' Didn't the continuity pull at him, draw him?

'Actually, love, I'm like Dad there at least, and you know he never could bear the place. He just liked the fact that he was a Selby of Chausey and could trace his roots back to the Norman invasion. He was the most appalling name-dropper; you must have noticed,' he said with wry affection.

Annie blinked. David hadn't cared for the house? Why hadn't she seen that? Name-dropper? Surely not!

He had been a sociable man and she hadn't been alone in being drawn by his brand of charisma. She'd been hostess to illustrious people—clever, witty people—David's friends—on the few occasions they'd entertained at home.

If it hadn't been for his illness she suspected that they would have socialised more, and travelled more too. Her husband had been greatly in demand for lecture tours, and an archaeological dig headed by him would never have lacked funds.

'Actually, Annie, I wasn't going to mention this but I've had an offer for the place and you'll never guess who from?' Wouldn't I? she thought bleakly, staring at his animated profile. 'And to be honest I could do with the capital right now. I've had this terrific offer. Annie?'

She put her smile back in place—the serene one that shielded the inner conflicts that were slicing through her. 'Tell me all about it,' she said obediently. She heard one word in ten, enough to tell her that what Nathan had indicated was in fact the truth. The cosy bubble she'd retreated into two years before had irretrievably burst.

Smiling and nodding, she began to wonder where the future would take her. Mostly the thought was frightening and the loss of her home was a dull ache, but she detected somewhere a small streak of excitement. . .

The first exam over, she avoided the post-mortem being held on the grassy lawn and skirted the building, her gown tucked into the bag slung over her shoulder. She was not sure whether she felt elated or depressed. Was complete amnesia concerning the pages she'd filled with neat, closely packed writing normal? For the life of her she couldn't recall a syllable of what she had written.

She cannoned into someone coming around the corner in the opposite direction. 'Sorry,' she gasped against a hard, unyielding wall of male chest.

The smile on her lips as she lifted her face towards the man who had caught her by the shoulders to steady her faded ludicrously when she recognised the unmistakable features of Nathan Audley. The three weeks which had elasped since she'd last seen him might just as easily have been thirty years; even then she would still have been able to recall the dark, hawkish features stamped with the indelible authority that cloaked his person. The impact of the hard, gleaming stare was more detrimental to her respiration than the impact of the clash of bodies. 'You!' she said accusingly.

Her eyes followed the line of the strong, stern jaw towards his mouth. Her heart began to pound at a relentless pace, making her head swim. He seemed to have plugged into all her vitality, draining it away like some sinister sorcerer. Insulation against the neat electric current of his slow, enigmatic smile and glittering eyes had vaporised.

The insane impulse to collapse weakly against the hard, masculine contours was hard to fight. Stop this, she told herself sternly. Think cabbage! It was an inspired thought—after all, who could think erotic thoughts if you filled your mind with cabbage? The absurdity of it did the trick and she dragged her eyes and body clear of the agonising contact.

'What are you doing here?' she heard herself demand quite truculently. By this point she knew she had imagined the languor that had invaded her body.

'In these hallowed precincts? Are you going to call the porter to have me ejected?' His eyes drifted over her, travelling over the cotton shirt that made her eyes seem more blue than grey, lingering over an unfastened button that hinted at the cleavage it concealed, before travelling to her slim hips and long legs encased in blue denim. 'The place is crowded with sightseers.'

'You're no tourist.'

'Just a trespasser,' he said cryptically. He reached out and flicked her cheek; the pad of his forefinger was faintly abrasive against her skin and she started as though shot.

His instinct was devastatingly accurate—a trespasser was exactly what he was. He'd trespassed into her life and in the space of twenty-four hours had caused ripples that were still sending their repercussive waves into her life. At home she had already begun to pack her belongings into neat cardboard boxes, though her personal possessions, when it came down to it, were meagre. She was only waiting now for the end of the exams. She comforted herself that the listing on the building would save it from wholesale destruction by its new owner.

'If you'd excuse me, Mr Audley,' she said haughtily, 'I'm in a hurry.'

'I noticed.' His body effectively blocked her path. Other than retracing her footsteps, she had no escape route. 'I'd like to look round the house, if it would be convenient.'

'Any time I'm not there.'

'Not gracious in defeat, are you?'

'Nothing you have done or said has influenced my decision,' she retorted, not caring much for his role of victor. 'Would you mind letting me pass? It's the house, not the sitting tenant you've bought.'

'Name the price.'

He was joking, though the shuttered, unblinking stare was too deep to decipher. All the same she tightened her jaw, which showed a tendency to gape, and smothered the surge of adrenalin that was neither pleasant nor unpleasant, just wildly stimulating. Her expression was derisive. 'Your humour borders on the bizarre.' Was he attempting to be insulting, or was he actually. . .?

'Am I laughing?' The air of outraged innocence was so absurdly inappropriate that she almost allowed herself to smile.

'What are you doing here?' she countered; the tension that was being generated was smothering and she sought refuge in the commonplace.

'I'm giving a guest lecture—economics.' He smiled at her expression of surprise. 'Formal education—or, rather, a lack of it—is forgiven when one has achieved a certain degree of success. You'd be amazed at how many honorary degrees and doctorates I've been offered from institutions who wouldn't have let me in the back door.'

'You refused them.'

He lifted a brow at her intuitive response. 'I don't carry excess baggage.'

He didn't expend any more energy on any single project than was required, she realised. His energies were focused, controlled—what would happen if he unleashed all his resources? she wondered, with a small internal shudder at the thought. 'That includes a family and the trappings that most of us want?'

'You want a family?' The faintest sneer lapped his words.

Annie flushed and drew herself up, regretting the fact that she'd allowed herself to be drawn into any discussion with him. 'I want to go home,' she said pointedly, looking somewhere over his shoulder. 'I've had an exam and I'm tired.'

'Did you follow in...your husband's footsteps? Archaeology?'

'History,' she said shortly, looking at her watch. As if he was interested! she thought wryly.

'I almost said "father" just then. I mean, it's usually the parents who have the guiding hand in grooming their offspring for future greatness. Following in Sugar Daddy's footsteps—quite touching really.'

Astutely, the words had been selected for their power to elicit a temptestuous response. His glance was almost gratified as he saw Annie's grey eyes glitter as if lit from inside her skull. The beacon of flame-bright curls seemed incandescent as she threw back her head, extending the long, slender neck. With a sharp flick of his wrist he interccpted the instinctive blow she aimed at him.

'Let me go!' she yelled, twisting her hand.

'Could it be that it's *you* that's embarrassed by the unorthodoxy of your marriage?' he suggested smilingly, controlling her struggles. The fist that came up to strike his chest stayed there imprisoned within his other hand.

'I married a dying man for his money and status,' she snarled. 'What is there to be embarrassed about? I'm as hard-faced as they come, remember,' she taunted. 'And if you don't let me go I'll scream the place down. That should look good in the Sunday scandal sheets— MILLIONAIRE ATTACKS WIDOW, POLICE INVOLVED.'

She was hitting back because his physical presence alone was making her desperate and his words only confirmed her suspicion that he had an uncanny knack of cutting to the bone of any subject. At the moment, when she was in the process of a major reassessment of her relationship in her defunct marriage, she wasn't prepared to have him dissect it clinically.

'Let's give them something to print, shall we?'

His mouth covered hers and she was immediately plunged into a maelstrom of uncontrolled ferocity. She hated with the same violent intensity as she hungered. How could each tiny movement of his mouth, his tongue, do such indescribable things to her?

He lifted his head and she was transfixed by the savage expression in his eyes. The upsurge of sensual hunger had lit specks of fire within the green; the effect was exotic. . .erotic. She felt her body sag against him.

The anticlimax and sense of deprivation when a group of Japanese tourists politely bowed their way past was incredibly powerful.

'What will they think?'

'They probably got a snap—the quaint Western mating ritual.'

'That's not funny.'

'Accurate. I want to see you.' He glanced at his watch, a faint frown creasing his forehead. 'We'll discuss it in. . .say, an hour at Chausey.'

His assumption that she would automatically submit to his autocratic decree made her temper spring into smouldering life. 'Discuss what? We have nothing to discuss. Besides,' she added, recalling her promise to spare a couple of hours for the kindergarten hit badly by the recent flu epidemic—originally she had intended to leave herself free to concentrate on the exams but she hadn't been able to refuse when asked by the desperate owner to step into the breach—'I have a previous appointment.' She didn't add that it was her part-time job that had previous call on her time.

The gleam in his eyes intensified and grew openly mocking as it dwelt on her bruised mouth and moved to the extra button that had come adrift on her blouse. 'You want reminding of what we need to discuss?' She only had time to blush fiercely. 'Make it this evening,' he said, and then he was turning away, his mind no doubt on some other, more pressing business, she decided bitterly.

She watched him go, her expression torn between longing and loathing. In the event, there was no winner. She finally gave a shuddering sigh as he disappeared from sight, and, noticing the state of her shirt, swiftly refastened it with defiance right up to the neck.

CHAPTER FOUR

'EXAMS getting to you, Annie?' The owner of the nursery, Maggie, watched her young helper with a frown of concern as the latter picked up the debris of toys which covered the carpeted floor.

Annie laughed as the toddler she had tucked against her hip placed a wet kiss against her neck and hit her over the head with a soft toy. 'Perhaps I'm coming down with flu,' she suggested, steering the subject away from personal channels.

'Don't, my dear, even suggest that... Without your help. . .' She gave a theatrical shudder.

'There is always the agency,' Annie reminded her. All the same, it was nice to be appreciated. . .needed, she thought wistfully. She loved being with the children and the atmosphere in this small establishment was intimate, warm. In her emotionally arid life she suspected that she needed them more than they did her, though the money she earned from it came in distinctly handy.

'But the children know you. . .you do have a knack,' the proprietress pointed out. 'You enjoy being with them and they know it; that sort of rapport is rare.' Her attention was diverted as the last parent arrived and Annie handed over her limpet-like charge.

'Go home, my dear; we'll finish up here.' The homely face of her employer creased into a rueful smile. 'I feel quite guilty taking advantage of your good nature like this, in the midst of your exams.'

Annie straightened up and unclipped the colourful overall from around her neck. 'What I don't know now. . .' She shrugged expressively. 'You know I love it here. Cloistered life can get a bit tedious. This helps keep a little balance in my life. Besides, I'm the perfect baby-sitter for my friend's kids with all this hands-on experience,' she said with a wry smile, thinking of her best friend who had recently produced a most delightful daughter.

'A great pity you didn't have children of your own,' the older woman said impulsively. 'Still, youth is on your side, as they say.'

I won't think about him, Annie told herself sternly. Less suitable father material would be difficult to conceive. 'I've seen how difficult it is for women to juggle a child and a career,' she observed neutrally.

'Don't believe the propaganda that says it's impossible. We see proof to the contrary here every day. Only don't leave it too late,' Maggie recommended.

'Do you still want me for a few hours on Friday, Maggie?' Annie asked, wondering uneasily whether something in her own demeanour had initiated this unusually forthright statement from the older woman. Has something about me changed? she wondered.

'If you can manage it, that would be tremendous.'

Annie nodded in acquiescence and waved her farewells. Walking back to the car, she felt the damp, sticky mark on her neck where the child had anointed her and smiled wistfully. With a shake of her head she increased her pace and derided herself for the yearnings that infiltrated her body so easily... Babies were great; it was fathers she had the problem with—at least, suitable ones, she reminded herself.

The slightly overgrown vegetable garden at Chausey had a therapeutic quality and after two hours of grubby labour Annie felt that some of the tension had seeped from her muscles. She straightened up and stretched the kinks from her spine, surveying the results of her efforts with a rueful frown. In David's time they had had a full-time gardener and part-time help; her occasional stint did little to alter the fact that nature was gradually reclaiming the cultivated order.

Ironically, exams which had for so long been her ultimate goal, had actually slipped into the back of her mind where the recent encounter with Nathan had relegated them. She tried unsuccessfully to prevent her thoughts returning to the already well-worn ground of the unsettling meeting.

No matter how violently she rejected her response to him she was unable to overcome her innate honesty and deny it. Disgust with herself curled in the pit of her belly. How was she capable of responding with such a wholesale lack of discrimination?

She was painfully aware that her sensual responsiveness had not escaped him, and he apparently felt inclined to explore the possibilities this opened up. She acknowledged the dilemma that that presented with an unconscious groan and tucked her hair behind her ears, her expression alternating between a dark frown and unfocused abstraction.

How to give a man like Nathan Audley—a man unscrupulous in achieving his desires—the brush-off was a problem she felt ill-equipped to deal with. He obviously imagined that she was as accustomed to casually satisfying her appetites as he was. In retrospect she regretted encouraging this misconception, but now was too late for regrets. What would he say if he knew the true state of affairs? she shuddered with mortification at the thought—the virginal siren!

Even if her well-founded dislike of the man hadn't been so strong she would never have contemplated the sort of affair that she glumly suspected he had in mind. She had retained an inbred and possibly unrealistic idealism which longed for a sincere, mutual commitment. A shallow, intense liaison was all this man wanted from her—all he and his ilk were capable of, she thought scornfully.

How was it possible, she wondered, to find a man so

loathsome and still be filled with this dull-edged, relent-less wanting? It was a compulsive sensation that refused to retreat to the dusty corner of her memory where she wished to consign it.

Instead, she found as she made her way back to the house that her breasts tingled and her thighs felt weak, not from the fierce stint of physical labour but more from a physical manifestation of her tortured thoughts. Damn the man, she thought as she shouldered her way into the kitchen, her hands full of the vegetables she'd picked from the kitchen garden.

'Dirty hands. You have an uncanny knack of surpris-ing me, Annie. I wouldn't have thought you were the type to ruin your manicure.'

'You!' She spun round, the fresh produce cascading from her arms on to the floor. Nathan was seated on the edge of the long, scrubbed pine table, watching her with a sphinx-like impassivity. Her fingernails, not painted scarlet and talon-like as he'd implied, cut into the flesh of her palms, inscribing half-moons; they were, fortunately for the tender flesh, short and neatly trimmed.

'A dirty face too,' he remarked. His expression grew overtly cynical as she flinched away from the finger he had intended to trace the smudge with.

'What do you think you are doing?' Her eyes hard-ened while her heart picked up its tempo. The quiver of recognition in her belly became a hot, writhing sensation. He looked offensively at ease in her home, she realised, angry with him and mortified by her response.

'Waiting for you.' He managed, she noticed, to look equally aloof in the open-necked polo shirt and casual, olive-coloured jeans as he did in more formal attire — tall, athletic, oozing vitality with a throw-away elegance which was uncontrived. 'We had an. . .appointment, if you recall.'

'I recall you issuing some sort of order,' she agreed.

'But I'm in the happy position of being able to ignore your decrees. You also happen to be trespassing; I've not been evicted yet,' she reminded him resentfully. This was her territory, if temporarily. How dared he invade it?

'Under the circumstances,' he responded drily, 'I took your compliance for granted.' The absinthe-coloured eyes, which had narrowed at her aggressive posture, glittered with satisfaction as she flushed hotly at this reminder. 'As for eviction, you were very fierce about me having no influence upon your decision. You can't have it both ways.'

His subtle amusement deepened at her angry confusion. 'You may be going to turn this place into some rich people's watering-hole, but right now it's still my home and I like my privacy.' Poor Chausey. When the choice had come down to it or Matthew there had been no competition, but she still felt as if she'd betrayed the old house.

'I can appreciate that,' he conceded. 'But I took your silence earlier to be an agreement. And if you want to keep your sanctum safe I suggest you lock the occasional door. I didn't even have to open this one, or use the keys Matt so kindly provided me with.'

Annie stared in appalled silence at the collection of keys he swung from his finger. 'Matthew had no right. . .' she began.

'Possession might be nine-tenths of the law but Matt is the vendor. And your period of squatter's rights is shortly to be terminated.'

She swallowed, determined not to allow him to see the mortification she felt. 'I'd have thought even you could have waited a couple of weeks,' she choked. 'I can't possibly stay here if you're going to be traipsing around with your tape-measure, mentally tearing down walls. I'll put up in a hotel until the exams are over.'

'You are well aware that the listing on the place precludes my tearing down anything. Besides, I came here to see you—as we both know—so why all the fencing?' He stood up and she willed herself not to retreat physically to combat the instinctive and appalling urge to gravitate towards him.

'I don't want to see you, talk to you, do. . .anything with you.' Hell, I'm panicking, she thought with an inward groan; I'm babbling like an idiot with the sophistication of a lollipop.

The green eyes were studying her with a clinical curiosity tinged with a layer of irritation as she groped for some vestige of serenity. 'I don't like you; I almost think I hate you,' she said in a low, urgent tone. 'I never intended to give the impression——'

He gave a low sound of vexation that cut across her faltering words. 'Come, Annie. The naïve, predictable denials are quite unnecessary between us. I'm not here because we like one another.' His darkly defined eyebrows rose in sardonic mockery. 'As for impressions, I'm aware that you are as attracted to me as I am to you. Good God, how can a woman of your experience and sexuality manage to look embarrassed?' he murmured critically. 'I don't waste time with meaningless polite conventions.'

'Thank you for explaining; I might have missed that,' she replied with faint but sparkling irony, finding black humour in this horrific situation which she was finding impossible to cope with. 'I can imagine that your sort of money must put you above the normal conventions.' She rubbed a hand distractedly over her face, spreading the dirt along the curve of her cheekbone. 'I take it that this is your quaint way of asking me to sleep with you? Tell me, does it usually work?' she asked, managing an incredulous tone.

'Beautiful things are usually flawed,' he remarked in an almost distracted voice, completely ignoring her response. 'But if I'd seen you like this the first time I might almost have believed you were the exception.

You don't look much like the practised seducer right
now.'

His eyes rested for a moment on her full, trembling
lips. Her bare skin had a translucent, glowing quality.
'Is that the secret of your success?' he asked, his voice
hard now, angry almost. 'The ultimate in deception. . .
I really do think you are the supreme example of a
particular type.'

She was glad of the anger; the low, gravelly, seductive
quality of the tone which had preceded it had made her
knees grow feeble and laid the foundations for a flood
of trembling weakness. 'I'm no victim, Mr Audley. If
that makes me a "type", so be it!' she replied huskily.

The compulsive way his eyes moved over her was
incredibly arousing, she discovered much to her horror
as her body reacted flagrantly to the touch as though it
had been his fingers stroking her skin. Her arms went
around herself in a consciously protective gesture. 'And
if I'm a "type" you so obviously despise I can't begin
to understand why you waste your time seeking me
out. You've made it quite clear that I can expect
nothing from you.' She gave a dismissive shrug. 'I have
more rewarding avenues to pursue.'

'I'm no victim either,' he replied coldly. Her words
had had the desired effect of alienating him completely,
but she gained little pleasure from the fact, just a
wrenching feeling of misery. 'Is that the problem? Do
you only sleep with men intoxicated enough by your
charms to give you what you want? I'm sure you'll find
compensations in my bed; I could make you forget all
the other men.'

She gave a small gasp of outrage. 'Are you implying
I sleep with men for money?' She chose to overlook his
confident claim because it opened up doors in her
consciousness—avenues of speculation she didn't
intend to explore. Nathan as a lover—the sensations
the thoughts conjured up made the room tilt on its axis
and she swiftly exiled the notion from her head.

'I'm sure you're far more subtle than that, Annie.'

Is that meant to placate me? she wondered incredulously, fury replacing her bemusement. 'Get out! Is that subtle enough for you?' she snapped, desperate by now for him to leave. It was all she could do to stop herself trembling visibly.

'Don't get me wrong; I'm not ungenerous as a lover, but I won't be manipulated, not by an avaricious little bounty-hunter, no matter how unusual and cruel her beauty happens to be.'

She covered her ears with her hands. 'Are you listening to me at all? I don't want to manipulate you, sleep with you, or even lay eyes on you again!'

His hands removed her clenched fists and held them in a loose grip at her sides. 'For once, Annie, do something because you want to, you need to, you *ache* to. I know you think you get a high from being in control, watching men tie themselves in knots to get your attention—and more. Allow yourself the luxury of pure self-indulgence; just follow your instincts.'

A sliver of emerald satisfaction, cold yet sensual, entered his eyes as a violent shudder rippled through her body, her eyes huge and clouded with fear and, yes, furtive excitement. 'I feel greedy when I look at you,' he disclosed huskily.

His hands, warm and strong, had moved to the curve of her waist; his fingers had actually discovered the small band of uncovered flesh between her jeans and top. A soft, silent, incredible explosion took place in the confines of her confused head and the hunger, the aching need, was too great to bear.

'Don't say that. . .' she pleaded in a small, breathy whisper. Her head fell backwards and with it the swath of her fiery hair. It felt too heavy for her neck to support; her bones were insubstantial things not equipped to hold her upright any longer.

Nathan was capable of holding her, though; even now he was drawing her pliant body closer to his. The heat of his body, the scent of him, unfamiliar but pleasing, was blotting out everything but the terrible craving and frustration which made her flesh burn.

'It's true,' his voice whispered across her skin, warm and enticing, the sound a source of further sensual torment. 'I wanted you the moment I saw you; I'm usually more discriminating, but. . .'

The words gave her the strength to pull away. 'In this case you're prepared to accept my flaws,' she gasped. She was tingling with an outrage that swept over her like a forest fire, from the tip of her fiery head to the end of her pearly toenails. 'Can a body bear such condescension?' she sneered wonderingly.

'You were bearing it quite successfully a moment ago,' he said with a languid hauteur that didn't quite slot together with the flared nostrils and the pulse that beat visibly in his jaw.

'But then think of all the practice I've had at pretending,' she said provocatively. The anger simmering in her veins was directed at both him—for offering her such supreme insults—and herself for being such an easy victim of his charismatic sensuality.

'I can distinguish between artifice and reality. . .that's what worries you,' he countered. 'You're not as predictable as I assumed at first.' The concession was murmured sibilantly from between clenched teeth.

'Is this a compliment?'

'But I wouldn't overplay the air of mystery,' he advised cryptically. 'Tantalise is very close to tedious, if employed injudiciously.'

'I have no wish to tantalise you or any other lecherous pig!' she spat back swiftly.

The smile had a volcanic quality, dormant but smoulderingly dangerous. 'I enjoy a challenge, but then I'm sure you realise that. However, it's pushing the bounds of credibility to suggest that what passed between us was some sort of assault. Despite your frenzied denials, Annie, you are as fascinated by the idea of being my mistress as——'

'Lover,' she countered automatically in a stunned voice, simply because she hated the old-fashioned image of the kept woman which the archaic word conjured up.

'You make a distinction?' he said, with an air of dry amusement at her foible.

'A purely academic one,' she said swiftly, just in case he had mistaken her interruption for acceptance of his arrant nonsense. 'You accuse me of being an amoral opportunist and in the next breath proposition me. What does that make you?'

'I am simply bringing out into the open what we've both known since we first met,' he said crisply. 'I was simply translating all this blistering sexual awareness into syllables we can both relate to. The way you live your life is nothing to me any longer. . . I have Chauscy, Matt has his freedom. I think our mutual hostility would fade considerably if we slept together.'

'I'll live with hostility, thank you.' His bluntness and perception were too acute for her liking, but he was wrong about one thing: she would always despise him.

'You distract me.'

'Should I apologise?' she said tensely. His eyes, smoky green, were examining her with all the warmth of a microscope lens.

'Why are you so scared of me, Annie?'

The soft question made the pupils in her wide eyes dilate violently. 'I'm not.' The conviction did not ring out as clearly and derisively as it was meant to. She bit her lower lip.

'Sex can be an excellent medium of expression. Also I am plagued by women whose mission in life appears to be to make themselves indispensable to me. . .'

'What a bore. . .' she drawled, blinking. He sounded so outrageously matter-of-fact; this ability to make the preposterous sound like acceptable normality was unnerving. She felt as if her discomposure and inexperience with such intimate subject matter were blazoned across her face.

'Am I supposed to be some talisman against these women panting to slide between your sheets, or more likely your cheque-book? Because let's face it, Nathan Audley, personality-wise you don't exactly ooze warmth.'

Her derision made absolutely no impact on his confidence, she realised, observing his impassive expression.

'Yet you continually tell me there's no future in the package for me,' she continued, almost breathless with frustrated fury. 'I find it pathetic that you expect me to be overwhelmed by a primitive, mindless desire for you and give my all,' she said sneeringly.

'Is that what you're afraid of?' he said softly as she stiffened, a disturbing gleam illuminating the topaz flecks in his eyes. 'I'm flattered.' To add insult to injury he grinned at her swift, inarticulate but eloquent display of outrage.

'I have matured past the point where the stimulation of a body, no matter how good, is sufficient to satisfy me. As beddable as you are I don't welcome the thought of being ruled by a purely physical response either. So possibly we are both in a similar situation. Advantages on both sides slightly outweigh any objections. You would prove a daunting prospect to any female on the make.'

He had to be the most cold-blooded, arrogant, smug. . . 'In other words a common little bimbo like me is not to your refined taste.' Her eyes, glittering with a dangerous cold fire, opened to their fullest. 'Why, I appreciate the full sacrifice now. . . I'm overwhelmed,' she trilled from between gritted teeth. 'Get out of here. . .now,' she said flatly, coldly. She was shaking with rage; the insult was insupportable.

'You're the one getting out,' he reminded her, breaking the tension-charged silence. 'I can't imagine why you're acting like some outraged virgin,' he mused, regarding her with half-closed eyes that were anything but sleepy. 'Do you have some aversion to the truth, Annie? Like your liaisons neatly packaged in sentimental platitudes, do you, sweetheart?'

'I like some warmth, some depth,' she replied, her voice fortunately steadier than her knees. 'Not a cold fish like you.' The lines bracketing the sensual curves of his mouth deepened, and his breath whistled out from between clenched teeth.

Why she should feel astonishment at the unbridled and immediate response that her words set in motion... They might, she would realise at a later, saner moment, have been devised to initiate it—the aggressive thrust of his tongue into the warm, honeyed recesses of her mouth, his body taut, shaken by a fine tremor that spoke volumes of the fierce control he still retained; her body was suffused by her impressions of the man who held her.

With a will of its own her limbs fought to fuse more closely with the predatory male who had an instanteously addictive quality.

The small, wrenching whimper was her own, she realised dazedly as he released her...put her from him. Her eyes were blank as she watched him run his fingers through his dark pelt of hair; the rapid rise and fall of his chest beneath the shirt which had come unbuttoned almost to his waist was swiftly brought under control. She recalled the texture of his hair-roughened skin beneath her questing fingers and made a small sound of horror.

Bleakly and with growing trepidation she realised that she had no such luxury—unlike him she couldn't switch off; the insistent sensations he had awoken were not so easily erased.

'Cold?'

She hit out blindly and missed his face by inches, her

arm moving in an arc through empty air. Her wrist was caught and held by iron fingers.

'What's wrong, Annie? Don't you like being controlled by sex? That's *your* prerogative, is it?'

She twisted her hand free, panting, frantically trying to marshal her defences. 'You're talking nonsense.'

He shrugged dismissively. 'I won't be controlled, Annie, not by the withholding of your favours or the reward. You will be mine, though,' he said with silky, deadly certainty. 'On my terms. I watched my father destroyed by a woman like you...she consumed him body and soul.' The green eyes shone with a loathing that made her want to protest her innocence as though she were this unknown woman. 'And, when it was all gone, she walked away. As is the way with your ilk.'

The sudden, soft-voiced attack, the animosity he exuded made her appreciate the depth of his dislike of her. It hurt. 'Maybe he thought it was worth it,' she replied slowly, the wide-eyed provocation deliberate.

'Are you?' A reluctant, hungry curiosity tautened the planes of his austere features.

'My price-tag is out of your reach. I've already told you that,' she derided, thinking of all the things she wanted—passion, a lasting involvement, things shared. 'Are you going?' She stood to one side of the still open door stiffly.

He regarded her unblinkingly. 'The next time the threshold will be mine, and you will be back where you started out. It might put things into a more realistic perspective.'

'I hope you'll show this building more respect than you do people,' she flung at him as he stepped out into the open air.

'I certainly shan't neglect it as you have,' he said derisively. 'My son will be living here.'

'I thought it was to be a hotel...' she said, unbalanced by this throw-away information. 'You can't have a son...you're not married.' Nathan—a father? she thought wildly. The two facts didn't jell. Her tone had been questioning; she was asking for confirmation, her voice tinged with a shade of alarm that he couldn't fail, with his uncanny perception, to pick up.

It didn't matter to her if he had a whole tribe of children and a regular harem, she told herself, but her composure wasn't just wavering, it was disintegrating about her feet. Nathan's personal life was nothing to her, she added with vicious denial, trying to escape from this shocked immobility which held her so firmly. . .trying to make her mind function with moderate poise.

'That is not a prerequisite,' he pointed out, his brooding contemplation observing her sudden confusion with every sign of malicious satisfaction. 'Or do I offend your high moral values?' he suggested sarcastically.

Son—he had a child. Was he a small version of the father? Green eyes minus the ingrained cynicism? She could recall clearly how Nathan had stated his rejection of marriage. . .what did the mother of his child think of that, or didn't she have a say in the matter?

Looking at the dark profile of her tormentor, she could well imagine that scenario; poor woman. Annie's sympathy was heartfelt but there was the puzzling, unexpected empty sensation in the pit of her stomach to account for. . .only she couldn't.

'Matthew never mentioned your son,' she said lightly, moistening her dry lips.

'Should he have?'

'I'm glad the place will be a home,' she said huskily. She was, even if *he* had to be the owner. Stupidly a rush of warm tears filled her eyes as a lump of emotion rose to clog her throat. Chausey was not to be a hotel; her worst fears would not see the light of day. . .where was the delight?

Fighting the conflicting emotions, she didn't see the fleeting expression that drew his dark brows together

in a fierce frown as though her sudden reaction had
perplexed him. 'Does that mean you'll be living here?'
she said suddenly, her expression openly appalled at
the prospect.

'I can see the prospect fills you with delight,' he said
drily. 'Wondering how long you can hold out?' he
taunted.

She flushed with anger. 'Don't hold your breath,' she
retorted childishly. 'Or rather do,' she added.

He strolled away laughing; he had an extremely
attractive laugh—warm, generous—all the things he
definitely wasn't. 'I had a proposition to put to you but
I can see you're not in a receptive frame of mind,' he
called to her. 'Next time.'

She rubbed the back of her neck where the flesh
tingled and closed the door, locking it this time. Proposition? Hadn't he made enough of those? It was the
lack of conviction in her own responses that dismayed
her—the fact that she had to work so ridiculously hard
to convince herself as well as him of her determination.

Automatically she retrieved the produce that lay
scattered across the floor. Her mind was in a turmoil.
One thing was sure though—she had to find somewhere
else to live; the gatehouse was out of the question given
this new information.

An awful thought occurred to her: what if that was
why he had allowed Matthew to keep the gatehouse
for her to live in? It had been an uncharacteristic
concession on his part. Had she all along been intended
as the mistress, handily located at the bottom of the
drive? she wondered cynically. Did the woman who
had borne his child accept his philandering with com-
plaisance, or did each affair hurt her?

Annie knew that, for her, total commitment, an
exclusivity would be a vital part of any relationship,
though sometimes, seeing couples around her, she
wondered whether she was being unrealistically romantic. Usually she was able to maintain her unreasonably

optimistic outlook no matter what life threw at her, but today. . .

All along she'd known that accepting the offer of the gatehouse had been a mistake; now she knew just how much of one it was. Going back never worked but the offer had given her a stopgap, a safe haven, and it had eased Matthew's concern over her future. She couldn't stomach living so close to Nathan and his family, watching them living in her home. A spasm of violent distaste contorted her features at the idea.

How easy it must be for him to dominate his prey, she thought, her mind conjuring up an instant image of the impossibly distinguished, dark, sensual features. Contemplating such a fate for herself was unthinkable, but how much longer could she hold back from the intense desire he had evoked with his untimely advent into her life?

Alone, she found it easy to see clearly the foolishness of even the briefest of affairs with him, but when he was in the room and she was bombarded, almost bewitched by the high-voltage vitality and sensuality of the man her conclusions were less firm.

No, Nathan Audley spelt jeopardy for her. She had to keep a safe distance and wait for her natural good sense to reassert itself; this temporary insanity had to fade, she decided with a touch of desperation.

Over the next two weeks anyone who noticed her loss of serenity attributed it to the ongoing examinations. As these were an affliction that most of her friends were sharing it was doubtful whether they noticed anything amiss, she realised, seeing a sea of pale, drawn faces around her. She felt as if she drifted through these momentous tests almost in a dream, strangely detached from them.

She saw nothing of Nathan and was glad of it—so why did she leap like a startled deer every time the phone or doorbell chimed? And was it only trepidation that made her heart-rate accelerate? She wished she could be sure. The flu-like symptoms were insidious, their onset almost imperceptible, but by the time she had finished her final exam just putting one step in front of the other seemed too much of an effort; every muscle in her body ached.

Tea, aspirins and an hour's nap in the armchair and she would be fine, she told herself with jaded optimism. Most of her belongings were temporarily in the gate-house; she only had the remnants of her occupation and herself to remove before Nathan took possession tomorrow. Head resting on the wing-back, she fell into a feverish sleep, muttering softly at frequent intervals as dreams troubled her.

The hand on her arm, roughly shaking her, was the next thing she was conscious of. 'David. . .?' Unfocused and dark-rimmed, her eyes reluctantly opened. She didn't hear the angry hiss as the man beside her heard her wistful murmur.

Angry green eyes, a dark, saturnine face swam into focus. She jerked upright and instantly regretted the motion. 'Go away; the place isn't yours until tomorrow.' Her voice emerged raspily from a dry sore throat.

'Thursday the twentieth is today,' he said, his glance encompassing the pallor of her skin and the disorientated, feverish gleam in her eyes. The effort of keeping her heavy-lidded eyes open seemed to be taking all her will-power. He touched the cold cup on the table beside her and examined the bottle of aspirin. 'I'd say you slept the clock around,' he continued as she regarded him with mute disbelief.

Annie groaned. 'Oh, no, I can't have. . .' Propelled by an urgency fuelled by the humiliating certainty that she was the trespasser and that he probably thought this was all an elaborate hoax to hold on to her tenure, she leapt from her seat. A sheen of perspiration broke out across her brow. Feebly she batted off his attempt to steady her as she swayed. 'I'm quite capable,' she said faintly.

'Of falling flat on your lovely face. . .though grey isn't really your colour,' he observed, his brows drawing into a straight line as he observed the blue discoloration around her lips. 'Sit down, woman,' he barked.

Indignant at being addressed in such stentorian accents but incapable of doing anything else, she subsided, despising the weakness in her legs. 'Don't worry; I'll be out of here in a minute. I might have a touch of flu,' she added cautiously by way of explanation.

'Dear God, don't tell me you're one of those martyrish women who struggle on regardless,' he said with disapproval. 'Matt rang me this morning to ask where the hell you'd disappeared to; he's been trying to contact you since yesterday.'

'I meant to ring him.' She rubbed her fuzzy head in frustration. 'I'll just get the rest of my stuff and leave you in possession.'

Why the hell did she feel so defensive? Just because he managed to make her sound inconsiderate and negligent. Probably he could make a good case for her being single-handedly responsible for the hole in the ozone layer, she decided bitterly. . . Paranoia—I'm cracking up, she decided wryly.

'Can't you round up one of your young men—Josh, wasn't it?—to help you? Or doesn't he care to be exposed to all those virulent microbes?'

'Josh is giving a paper in. . .' She shook her head, trying to penetrate the cotton-wool blanket that made her mental processes slow and sluggish. 'Stockholm, I think,' she said vaguely. 'I'm more than capable——' she began; he obviously wanted to see the back of her as quickly as possible.

'So you mentioned,' he interrupted drily. 'Why didn't you call a doctor?'

'It's just a cold,' she protested, trying to marshal her reserves to get to her feet. The last thing she had

wanted was to have her farewell to the home she loved
so deeply witnessed by anyone—especially this man;
the poignancy would be made into a snide joke by his
derision. . . How had she slept for so long?

'Let's let the doctor decide, shall we?'

'What are you doing?'

'Who's your GP?' he asked tersely, ignoring her
query completely. 'You might as well tell me because
you're not getting out of here until you've had a
thorough check.'

'I didn't think you cared,' she sneered.

A dark brow shot up. 'I'm thinking of the bad
publicity if you manage to do yourself further harm. It
would be fodder for the people who devise lurid
headlines. I can see myself cast in the role of Victorian
villain, casting the sweet heroine out in the cold. These
people need very few solid facts to sustain them. I'm
sure that, given financial incentive, you could be quite
inventive.'

Closing her eyes after casting him a look of loathing,
she sank back into the chair and gave him the information. She felt too terrible to persist in her obstinacy.
Every inch of her body ached terribly and her throat
suffered every time she swallowed, let alone spoke.

'You care about your image, then, do you?' she
taunted hoarsely. 'And here was I thinking you were a
law unto yourself.'

His green eyes touched her with contempt as he
pressed the buttons on the telephone receiver. 'Since
my son began to read newspapers and listen to the
media I have done. The last time my name was
plastered across the dailies he had nightmares for a
month,' he informed her coldly.

Feeling like a small child castigated for a smart
remark, and angry at the sensation of guilt, her
expression grew mutinously truculent. His concern for
his son made her realise how little she knew this man—
a situation that was not fated to alter. On the periph-

ery—that was the only place he would ever want her. An irrational sense of tremendous loss rose like a wave in her throat, threatening to overwhelm her.

'He won't come out at this time of day—you have to ring earlier,' she remarked, trying to escape the spiralling blast of emotion. She spoke from experience; doctors' visits and calls to the surgery had been a way of life not so long ago.

Nathan just smiled with silky confidence, and Annie watched, waiting to see him deflated by an encounter with the league of impregnable receptionists who guarded the doctors with efficient zeal.

He was impressive, she had to admit; his charm, even when disembodied down a telephone, was nothing short of devastating. She detected no attempts to fob him off and could almost hear the grovelling at the other end of the line—disgusting!

'Half an hour,' he announced.

She closed her eyes. 'It's a total waste of time.'

'Unlike suffering in stoical silence—a common tactic for attention-seekers.'

'I'm not an attention-seeker,' she protested. Tears—God, I must be sicker than I thought, she decided with dismay, trying to blot the slow cascade with the back of her hand. 'I hope you catch it, you unsympathetic pig,' she added with deep sincerity.

The growl of deep laughter reinforced his heartless nature, she decided. 'That's far preferable to your impression of an early Christian martyr,' he approved, a smile still curving his mouth as he met her outraged glare. 'Spitting fire and brimstone is much more you, angel. Now sit there like a good little girl.'

'I am neither little nor——'

'Good,' he supplied with a shrug. 'That fact has already been established,' he said drily. 'I have to ring my architect who was due to meet me here this afternoon.'

'You don't let the grass grow, do you?' she said

bitterly. 'There's a phone here,' she pointed out as he stood there, his hand on the door-handle.

'I'll use my mobile, thank you.'

'I'm not big on industrial espionage,' she grated.

'A resourceful girl like you is a fast learner, I feel certain.'

'There speaks a sore loser,' she muttered, a flame of colour alleviating the pallor of her skin.

'Would you mind elaborating?'

The silky tone made her look up in surprise—he would have superhuman hearing; he could probably see in the dark too. 'I mean,' she said in a painful, husky drawl, refusing to be overawed by his silkily dangerous regard, 'that you are being especially insulting to me because I had the temerity to refuse an invitation into your bed.'

'That subject is a long way from being resolved, I think you'll find. As for my being insulting, Annie, I wasn't giving you any special treatment,' he drawled. 'I think you might be in danger of overestimating your significance in the scheme of things; beautiful redheads are fairly low on my list of priorities.'

With that cutting remark he left the room. I will not cry, she told herself, gritting her teeth, her face a mask of concentration.

The doctor was prompt, and he treated her with brisk familiarity. During the terminal stages of David's illness he had been instrumental in devising a regime of pain relief which had made the last days considerably more bearable for them both.

He examined her thoroughly, asked a few pertinent questions and regarded her quizzically over half-moon spectacles. A knock on the door, to which he responded, stopped the onset of the lecture she was steeling herself for.

Nathan entered the room, though why Annie was at a loss to understand. The two men began to discuss her as though she weren't there. She listened with growing incredulous anger as terms such as 'exacerbated by exhaustion' and 'complete rest' were bandied around with gay abandon.

'I'd be obliged, Dr Gregory, if you'd discuss my symptoms with me. I am neither dumb nor totally. . .' She grunted as she pulled herself upright on the sofa she had lain on for the examination. 'Stop fussing,' she hissed as Nathan assisted.

'You make a very tetchy patient, darling,' he observed as she violently shrugged off his arm. One eyebrow shot skywards as her vicious rebuttal was obliterated by a violent bout of coughing.

'Unless you want to end up in hospital, young lady, I suggest you start accepting a little help from your friends. Stubborn independence can be taken to extremes,' the doctor observed disapprovingly.

Annie looked from one man to the other, feeling a deep sense of helplessness. The gleam in Nathan's eyes taunted her to deny the friendship the medic had obviously assumed existed. . .

Friend! The irony was bitter. He was her enemy, she the synthesis of everything he despised in a female; she had been neatly categorised. The fact that he desired her was a reminder of human weakness which she suspected he didn't admit to very often. Yes, he loathed her, yet he was helping her. Her mind struggled to discover the hidden agenda behind this behaviour.

'I really don't feel too bad now.' Her voice held a placatory note, alive to the threat of hospitalisation.

'Don't wheedle, woman; I mean what I say. I thought you had more common sense than to neglect yourself in this ridiculous manner.'

'Perhaps we should let her sleep, Doctor.' Surprisingly Nathan rescued her from the remonstrances. 'I'll make you a cup of tea and you can tell me what she needs.' He sounded so solid and trustworthy that she wasn't surprised that the doctor accepted the suggestion without query. Why, she wondered, couldn't everyone else see how detrimental to her health Nathan Audley was?

Ignoring her aching limbs, she stood up shakily. The rest of her things were piled in the inner hallway; she was going to escape while the going was good, she decided with feverish determination.

CHAPTER FIVE

'GOING somewhere?'

Annie straightened up—too quickly; the hallway lurched and took several seconds to right itself. She could feel the cold sweat that clammily sprang out all over her skin; it made her light cotton T-shirt cling to the outline of her breasts, a fact she was blissfully unaware of.

It was the tight sensation when she tried to breathe that was preoccupying her at that moment; whether this condition could be solely attributed to the influenza bug she wasn't entirely sure. The predatory magnificence of the new owner of Chausey could have been a factor, she glumly admitted to herself.

'Yes.' Her defiant reply emerged as a croak and he watched her, leaning casually against the jamb of the door, effectively blocking her exit. 'I'm going to the gatehouse.' He had just better not try to argue with her, she decided belligerently. She tried to subdue another cough and picked up a cardboard box containing some of her treasures.

'Good idea.'

This deflating reply, which had been exactly the response she had hoped for, made her throat tight with tears of self-pity. He couldn't wait to get rid of her, could he? she thought bitterly. 'I don't suppose I'm very beddable, am I, like this?' She closed her eyes and muttered something viciously insulting about her own intellectual capacity. 'I think I'm probably delirious.'

'Melodramatic and inaccurate.' Her eyes shot open as she realised that her last comment had unintentionally been aired for public consumption. He had moved closer in a very purposeful and worrying way. 'On both counts.'

She instinctively hugged the box to her bosom as if it were a life-jacket. Not relinquishing it to him was suddenly inordinately important. 'I don't need any help from you; I'd prefer to starve in the gutter.'

'An unlikely scenario,' he murmured, the corner of his mouth lifting in ironic humour. 'However, if you feel the need to carry your clutter, fine,' he said agreeably as he scooped her and her treasures into his arms. His attitude spoke of an adult humouring a truculent and unreasonable child.

Annie issued a small strangled shriek of outrage. 'Put me down this instant,' she squeaked, ignoring the insidious attraction of the warmth and masculine fragrance drifting from his body while he coped with her hardly diminutive frame with surprising ease. 'I hope you don't think I find this nauseating display of macho domination appealing.'

The hair on his neck terminated in unruly curls, she noticed, oddly fascinated by the detail. He had a good neck—strong. . .good, clean lines like the rest of him.

'Shut up, there's a good girl, and indulge me.' She closed her eyes as his breath brushed her cheek, feeling even more light-headed. 'I promise you, if I were into entertaining fantasies about sweeping a woman off her feet, she wouldn't have a red nose or bloodshot eyes, and she'd definitely be inclined towards the ethereal.' He grunted as he began the ascent of the stone steps which led to the courtyard where his car was parked. 'Amazons are bad for the back.'

She feebly allowed herself to be placed in the rear of the car. 'I'm not fat,' she managed lethargically as he pushed the carton in beside her.

'How like a female to be concerned with her figure when she can barely walk.'

'You're the one who's been preoccupied with my figure,' she spat back, disgruntled.

'I seriously doubt whether I'm alone,' he said harshly, before closing the door on her.

Annie closed her eyes. 'I suppose you hold me personally responsible for my shape too,' she muttered half to herself.

The engine purred into instant life and her eyes met his in the rear-view mirror. 'In some ways I can see why you utilise it—in a world where the odds are stacked against females in the workplace. I've seen it done in quite exalted circles. You just don't have a workplace—unless we're talking beds, that is. I'm sure you're very professional at what you do.'

She grew light-headed with a dark anger that coursed through her feverish body as she listened to this cold assessment. 'I'm sure that as a man of above average intelligence you're aware of how much your father's marriage has tainted and distorted your view of relationships, but you have no right to treat me as though I'm some opportunist little tramp. I've asked nothing of you and I never will,' she said, her hoarse voice trembling with emotion.

'I just feel sorry for the child raised by a man with such a warped outlook on life...you're crippled by your own prejudices.'

'When I require your opinion I'll request it. It's always a mistake to pass judgement on subjects on which you have scant information,' he said grimly. His eyes gleamed with icy contempt as they momentarily raked her dishevelled figure.

'I see,' she muttered belligerently, feeling too ill to be temperate at that moment. The fact that he had drawn rapid and inaccurate sketches of her personality from the moment—no, even before—they'd met filled her with a crusading sense of injustice! 'So it's all right for you to issue the definitive study of my character or lack of it, but I'm to remain dumb in the presence of such an illustrious figure of perfection.'

The car squealed to a stop with a flurry of gravel that

hit the window against which her aching head rested.
'My son and his welfare are none of your concern,' he
said, inclining his head to fix her with a cold and hostile
gaze. 'He is not going to be exposed to a woman like
you until he's old enough not to have any illusions. It
takes a certain detachment to glimpse the real you
beneath the attractively wrapped exterior.'

The pain was sudden and vicious; it sliced through
her like a blade and surprisingly she knew that part of
the sorrow she was experiencing was reserved for the
father and his unknown son.

'Or any woman,' she said huskily, her expression
melancholy. 'What about his mother? Doesn't she have
any say in the matter?' She was glad that he couldn't
see her face, see the intensity of her interest betrayed
in that careless moment; her unhealthy interest in that
subject was becoming a real problem, she decided.

'His mother preferred money to the inconvenience
of a small child.' His eyes narrowed. 'Why so shocked,
Annie? I'd have thought you would have understood
such a transaction.'

'You can't buy a child,' she said, abhorrence in her
wide eyes and the twist of her lips. Did he actually
think her the sort of person who could trade a life—
her own or, even worse, her child's—for money?

The intense curiosity which she had been unable to
quell since she had known that an anonymous woman
existed who had borne his child fed greedily on this
awful information; the notion of any woman turning
her back on Nathan, let alone their child, troubled her
greatly. Or was it the knowledge that walking away
from even such a tenuous link as existed between her
and Nathan was causing her so much pain. . .?

But the two situations were not comparable, she
knew, and also knew that she didn't possess the
strength, or weakness, of the other woman.

'You can buy any commodity,' he said callously, the
lines between his eyes deepening as he took in her

expression of horror and loathing. 'Isn't that the principle you live by? I'm sure that given a similar situation you would have had no qualms about using the same tactics; in fact, I'm sure you would have been more imaginative.'

Annie permitted herself to be manhandled out of the vehicle. She felt too sick in body and spirit to fight any longer; the evidence of his brutal cynicism had somehow sapped the last remnants of resistance in her.

The small gatehouse, which had been bright and cheerful in the happy days when her aunt had occupied it, seemed empty and cramped after the space she'd grown accustomed to.

'Thank you.' Good manners rather than sentiment brought the words to her lips.

Looking around him with what she interpreted as a patronising frown, he placed her upon her feet. 'It's damp,' he said in an accusing tone. 'You can't propose to stay here.'

'Just as well you didn't buy it, then.' She made an impatient gesture and coughed drily. 'Will you go away? I've no intention of staying here any longer than necessary. I don't want you as a neighbour.'

Sleep—that was what she needed right now, and blissful solitude—no more Nathan and his ability to wound her. She put her hand on the smooth banister which ran the length of the steeply rising staircase that led from the sitting-room to the two small bedrooms.

'Got our next victim lined up?'

'That's a trade secret,' she said hollowly, not allowing him to see the pain he could so casually inflict. Later she'd have to analyse this ability. . .much later, though. Now all she wanted to do was crawl into some quiet corner.

He stood watching her slow, stiff-backed progress up the stairs in silence. It was obvious from the careful way in which she moved that each step cost her considerable effort but she was stubbornly determined not to let it show. A gleam of reluctant admiration entered his eyes as she reached the top.

Their eyes met and Annie felt the sudden pricking of tears. The warmth, the almost caressing humour that had slid into the cold green depths had obviously been a product of her fever, but for a moment she had felt drawn towards the tenderness.

He turned and was gone almost before she had remonstrated with herself for such irrational, whimsical behaviour. Rushing into Nathan's arms for comfort? Her brain must have taken leave of absence.

The roughly made bed was cold and unwelcoming, and it took her some time to remove her outer garments and crawl beneath the covers. She slept fitfully, shaken by bouts of shivering and intermittent racking coughs.

Later, half asleep, she opened her eyes and examined the cracks in the ceiling around the darkening patch where the roof had leaked last winter; she had never stretched the budget to get it repaired. Nathan was right about one thing—the place needed a sharp influx of cash; it was in a shameful state.

'Are you real, or am I hallucinating?' she enquired as she turned her head. 'You left.'

'I came back.' The hand that touched her forehead was clinical. 'The doctor left a cocktail of prescriptions to be filled.'

'You shouldn't have bothered,' emerged hoarsely from her dry lips.

'Possibly not, but I have this warm and generous nature that impels me to make chivalrous gestures,' he drawled.

'Only when you have an audience,' she snarled, plucking at the bedcovers with fingers that were not quite steady.

She didn't actually believe her indictment. Whatever else Nathan was, he was unapologetically himself. She couldn't imagine him exerting himself to impress anyone with pretty manners and cozening speeches; the man was abrasively arrogant and assumed that the rest of the populace would fall into line with him.

So why was he putting himself out to be kind to her? The worrying puzzle brought a frown to her wide brow.

'I don't think you're in a position to criticise,' he observed drily, his eyes following the chaos that her restless fingers were making of her hair, which lay in wild confusion on the pillow. 'I'm your guardian angel; all I have to do is inform your doctor friend how uncooperative you're being and he'll whisk you off into hospital.'

Frustration simmered inside her as she refused to release the tears that welled up. 'I hate hospitals.' The smell, the memories—her stomach tied itself in familiar knots and she fought to quell the irrational but instinctive panic. She closed her eyes, unwilling, frightened almost, to permit him to see the depth of her vulnerability. 'Give me the bloody tablets or whatever and go and do whatever it is that clever little millionaires do.'

His silent appraisal made her uneasily certain that he had seen everything she had been desperate to hide. Those green eyes, glitteringly alert and totally lacking compassion, caught her truculent, fever-glazed glare. The furrow etched between his brows had deepened as she'd mentioned his financial state and a film of icy disdain now clouded the emerald clarity.

'Sit up; you can't breathe down there.' Amazingly, no punitive remark. She blinked in tired confusion as he lifted her, his hands beneath her armpits, up the bed. A hand in the small of her back supported her weight as he rearranged her pillows. The pressure exerted by one finger sent her back against the soft support.

She was too surprised by the impersonal competence to do anything other than hold out her hand obediently when he went to place a selection of pills in her palm.

'Antibiotic, and something to lower your temperature,' he explained, putting a glass of cool fruit juice in her other hand. 'There,' he observed as she swallowed. 'Not so difficult when we dispense with the temper, is it?'

She banged the glass down noisily on the small bureau beside the bed. 'I didn't ask for your help; you're the last person I want to help me.' What form was he hoping her gratitude would take? she wondered with cynical distaste.

'You keep making these grand sweeping declarations, Annie. Don't you find it a perilous thing to do? It awakens a strong desire to make you swallow every syllable. . .an indigestible meal for anyone as pigheaded and stubborn as you.'

He picked up the jug off the bureau and refilled the glass. 'Drink plenty. . .the doctor's orders, not mine, if that makes rebellion less predictable,' he said with contemptuous irony.

Annie, bleary-eyed and incredibly weary, decided that he was fast losing patience with the situation. . . with her. Whatever he had hoped to gain from this extravagantly neighbourly gesture she was sure he was doomed to be disappointed. Her brain was too numb with fatigue and overwrought emotion to function beyond a basic level. Nathan's sinister motives were beyond her understanding. 'I suppose I should thank you,' she said gruffly.

'I've never played nursemaid before.' A faint, elusive smile lurked around his sculpted lips; the action made her belatedly aware that she'd been staring at the sensual outline.

'Not even to your son?' she asked, turning her head to find a cool spot on the pillow and hide the slow, dull colour that had washed over her fair skin. This bizarre fascination he inspired in her had a searing, spontaneous quality which even in her present miserable condition could terrify her.

'Other people who are far more competent have usually been on hand to do that.'

Tiredness was sweeping over her in a great wave and she fought to keep her eyelids open. 'Perhaps he wanted *you*,' she suggested sleepily.

'Unlike you.'

'You're not my father,' she pointed out drily. She'd just rest her eyes for a moment, she decided as the battle to keep them open grew too tedious.

'A biological impossibility...from a mathematical standpoint. Neither am I in the habit of substituting,' he said sardonically. His expression was grim as his gaze was drawn to her closed eyelids, delicate almost to the point of transparency, the blue tracery of veins visible beneath the delicate skin. Her eyelashes fluttered against the curve of her cheek but her eyes remained closed.

'I don't need a father substitute.' The words emerged softly but quite distinctly. 'Been there, done that.' Self-mockery, which was in danger of disturbing the neat category he had slotted her into, gave her final statement an impression of deep pathos.

Nathan stood there at the bedside for a moment; his expression had lost some of the insolent aggression which had dominated it moments before. The insulating urbanity peeled away and his chiselled features were drawn by a reluctant hunger into a tense, still mask. With an abruptness that didn't begin to hint at the internal battles being waged he turned on his heel and left the room, his long-legged, soft-footed stride inaudible.

Annie emerged slowly and reluctantly from the semi-comatose state that had made her half aware of the unfamiliar but somehow not strange surroundings. Then she remembered; she had slipped back to a time which could never be recaptured—a time of innocence she suddenly longed for as the dull ache, which seemed perpetually to inhabit the region behind her breast-bone, flared into life.

Her recall of the past hours—how many?—was hazy, dreamlike, but the memory of being woken and reluctantly swallowing cool liquid pressed to her lips was relatively clear. Tablets too she had forced past her raw throat. Experimentally she stretched her limbs. Better—a lot better, she realised with some relief.

She sat up in bed abruptly, the crumpled sheet slipping down to her waist. Nathan had been here; how long? The light streaming in through the window made it clear that she'd once again slept the clock around. What motivation could have induced him to adopt such a menial role? she wondered, all her senses alerted to the danger which she instinctively felt these extraordinary circumstances must bespeak.

She shivered, her hands rubbing the skin of her upper arms. Her eyes slid down to the camisole she had stripped down to before climbing into bed—innocently cotton but remarkably revealing. The deep sense of vulnerability increased tenfold at the thought of being completely and totally defenceless.

She searched her incomplete, fragmentary memories of the past twenty-four hours, trying to remember any indiscretions which might have passed her lips. With a sound of frustration she flung aside the bedclothes and swung her legs over the edge.

Thighs, long and smooth, stretched as she flexed her ankles in front of her. A half-dreamy, reflective expression entered her eyes as she stared at herself. Had he too looked at her creamy skin? A tingling sensation ran along her nerve-endings and, dry-throated, she licked her lips.

She made a sudden, almost silent noise of alarm and her lips parted in a silent sigh as she realised how just the thought of the man could make her slide into some sort of sensual limbo. Pull yourself together, Annie, she advised herself firmly.

NO RISK, NO OBLIGATION TO BUY... NOW OR EVER!

CASINO JUBILEE

"Scratch'n Match" Game

Here's how to play:

1. Peel off label from front cover. Place it in the space provided opposite. With a coin carefully scratch away the silver box. This makes you eligible to receive two or more free books, and possibly another gift, depending upon what is revealed beneath the scratch-off area.

2. Send back this card and you'll receive specially selected Mills & Boon Romances. These books have a cover price of £1.99 each, but they are yours to keep absolutely free.

3. There's no catch. You're under no obligation to buy anything. We charge nothing for your first shipment. And you don't have to make any minimum number of purchases - not even one!

4. The fact is thousands of readers enjoy receiving books by mail from the Reader Service, at least a month before they're available in the shops. They like the convenience of home delivery, and there is no extra charge for postage and packing.

5. We hope that after receiving your free books you'll want to remain a subscriber. But the choice is yours - to continue or cancel, anytime at all! So why not take up our invitation, with no risk of any kind. You'll be glad you did!

*Prices subject to change without notice.

YOURS FREE!

You'll look like a million dollars when you wear this elegant necklace! It's cobra link chain is a generous 18" long and its lustrous simulated pearl is mounted in an attractive pendant.

(Pictured larger to show detail)

CASINO JUBILEE
"Scratch'n Match" Game

SCRATCH HERE ?

PLACE LABEL HERE

CHECK CLAIM CHART BELOW
FOR YOUR FREE GIFTS!

2A6R

YES! I have placed my label from the front cover in the space provided above and scratched away the silver box. Please send me all the gifts for which I qualify. I understand that I am under no obligation to purchase any books, as explained on the back and on the opposite page. I am over 18 years of age.

BLOCK CAPITALS PLEASE

MS/MRS/MISS/MR _____

ADDRESS _____

_____

_____ POSTCODE _____

CASINO JUBILEE CLAIM CHART			
🍒	🍒	🍒	WORTH 4 FREE BOOKS A FREE NECKLACE AND MYSTERY GIFT
🍒	🔔	🍒	WORTH 4 FREE BOOKS
🔔	🔔	🍒	WORTH 3 FREE BOOKS CLAIM N° 1,528

MILLS & BOON READER SERVICE: HERE'S HOW IT WORKS

Accepting free books puts you under no obligation to buy anything. You may keep the books and gifts and return the invoice marked "cancel". If we don't hear from you, about a month later we will send you 4 additional books and invoice you for just £1.99* each. That's the complete price, there is no extra charge for postage and packing. You may cancel at any time, otherwise every month we'll send you 4 more books, which you may either purchase or return - the choice is yours. *Terms and prices subject to change without notice.

Mills & Boon Reader Service

FREEPOST

Croydon

Surrey

CR9 3WZ

NO
STAMP
NEEDED

She glanced at the bottle of antibiotics and read the instructions. Unfortunately she had no idea when her last dose had been administered. Pity her unwelcome nurse hadn't thought to leave a note with the relevant information, she thought, nurturing a sense of injustice which she knew, under the circumstances, was ill-placed. Still, anger was easier to cope with than her earlier speculation.

The T-shirt that she found neatly folded over a chair barely reached the top of her thighs but she didn't give it a thought as she padded barefoot downstairs.

She blinked and froze in shock at the foot of the stairs. The door to the small, galley-type kitchen stood open and a tall figure beyond was lighting the gas stove, his dark head bent as he placed a kettle on the flame.

'I heard you moving around,' he said without moving his head, apparently able to sense her steady, horror-struck gaze. 'How are you feeling?'

'What are you doing here?' Her voice had a strident, accusing quality that grated on her own ears.

He took two steps which took him into the sitting-room. 'Amnesia?' he suggested, with a quirk of one dark brow. 'I knew you'd be grateful for my minis-trations.' His expression was impassive except for the odd, glittering light in his eyes as they swept over her, slowly taking in every detail—or so it seemed to her—from the fiery nimbus of tumbled curls to the shapely length of her legs which emerged from the shirt.

Annie tried with every ounce of her considerable will-power to appear unmoved by the scrutiny but, to her intense shame, she felt the hardened peaks of her breasts thrust against the thin fabric that covered them. Green eyes slid back to her face and she knew that no detail had gone unnoticed. Her teeth dug into the flesh of her full lower lip as she tried to combat the heart-thudding, suffocating sensation that made her head swim.

'I was in no position to actively seek your help. . .or prevent it.'

His dark features transformed into a thin-lipped smile that she mentally tagged as demonic. 'Is that why you look so suspicious? You imagine I took advantage of your unconscious state to slake my lust?' he said with a blighting contempt that brought two dull patches of colour to the crests of her high-slanted cheekbones.

'Let me reassure you that I prefer my partners to remember the event. Though in your case I imagine that the faces tend to become interchangeable. You'll remember me,' he promised darkly, his eyes sliding with insulting deliberation over her body.

The outrageous slur enabled her to pull free with a surge of adrenalin. She shook back her heavy mane of hair and stalked into the room, hands on her hips.

'I'll forgo that pleasure and take your word for it,' she said drily, a small, insulting smile playing around her mouth. 'The way your turgid mind is apparently stimulated by my alleged promiscuity does not lead me to explore the accuracy of your little-boy boast. Even the size of your bank balance would be insufficient inducement.'

The acrid taste in her mouth was awful as she tried to steady her trembling knees—a symptom of the flu, she told herself sensibly. He wanted to demean her—everything he did, said was aimed at that ultimate goal. How could she be so physically responsive to such a hateful man? she wondered, close to despair.

The narrowed green eyes glittered like shards of transparent crystal. 'We'll get back to my boasts shortly,' he promised silkily, his deep voice a sensual purr that was like a fingertip stroking the nape of her neck. 'Am I to infer from your embittered little speech that that ripe little body is inhabited by a paragon of virtue and not an amoral little bitch?'

The virulence in his voice lashed out at her like a blow. 'I'm not about to defend myself to you,' she said flatly. How could she? In his mind her guilt had been assigned before he had laid eyes on her. 'But whatever you think of me you must admit that I have a modicum of discrimination—I have managed not to fall into your arms.'

She watched with reluctant fascination as his long fingers—extraordinarily elegant, shapely fingers—flexed and extended; she could imagine them curling around her own neck, where she suspected, from the menacing expression on his face, he wanted to place them.

'The only reason you shrink from me when with every fibre of your being you want...crave my touch——' he gave a sinister smile as she visibly paled, her eyes filled with a haunted apprehension '—is that I know you for what you are,' he continued, ignoring her soft sound of denial.

'Men never look beyond the simmering sensuality you radiate, do they, Annie? God gave you a beautiful body and an enviable intelligence—missed out on the soul, though, didn't he?'

He was pale; she could see the muscles bunching beneath the fabric of his shirt as he continued to feed the fury that was consuming him.

'You like to blind men, see them helpless, infatuated by the promise of youthful sensuality. He was old enough to be your father.'

'I loved David!' she screamed.

'Love!' he sneered. 'He couldn't have been capable of satisfying you. I suppose you were faithful even when he was an invalid,' he mocked. 'I might have believed that if I hadn't seen firsthand how responsive you are, Annie. Because, honey, you are good. The best the old fool could have hoped for was discretion.' His smile was one of triumphant disgust as guilty colour spread slowly over her skin.

Annie knew he was misinterpreting her reaction but for a split-second she had thought that somehow he knew about the hollow nature of her marriage, the fact that it had never been consummated. It was something she felt strangely responsible for, as if, despite the facts to the contrary, she had in some way been lacking. Had David fostered this irrational. . .? She blinked, shocked at this mental display of disloyalty.

'A heart attack killed my father.' His tone was changed, grown almost conversational, flat, devoid of the previous passion, and somehow even more alarming. 'But my stepmother was the catalyst. She bewitched him, bankrupted him and when he began to realise just what a fool he'd been she completed the job by cuckolding him. Why, she even tried to seduce me. I often wondered whether you and Matt——'

'Bastard!' She hit out wildly, his supercilious smile almost as hateful as the unforgivably prurient speculation he'd voiced. Her blow was fielded and her arm anchored against his side, the action dragging her closer. 'You're sick. . .' she accused, panting as she tried to pull away.

'You *were* sick, remember?' he taunted. 'And alone; doesn't that tell you anything?'

'You make me sick,' she gasped. 'I'd prefer to die than be beholden to you.'

'Maybe you would have died, but then I hardly think that the sort of deep, meaningful relationships you indulge in inspire the tender side of your partners. They were scarcely queuing up to wipe your fevered brow.'

'That's me—good for a tumble in the hay and nothing else.'

'You said it, honey, and don't look so outraged; you make the rules, you play by them.'

She twisted her wrist, and winced as his fingers didn't relinquish their iron grip. 'Was I meant to be grateful for your white knight act?' she goaded. 'It was hardly high drama, was it? People don't die of flu very often. Is that what all this is about, Nathan? You're piqued because even after all this effort someone as easy as me can't stand the sight of you?'

One violent movement, which almost made her feet leave the ground, pulled her to him. A hand in her hair pulled her head back, forcing her to accept the punitive swoop of his mouth. She closed her eyes, feeling blinded by the expression that glittered in his eyes. It was an embrace inspired by hate, dark and dizzy, but a great chasm of trembling weakness and compliance opened up and she fell headlong into it.

Obedient to the demands being made, her lips opened wider, welcoming, hungry for the invasive thrust of his tongue. His heart pounded against her aching breasts. The unbearably intoxicating sensation made her body arch with an aching need for fulfilment; capitulation took command of her actions. Hands linked together at her hips, fingers splayed into the small of her back, Nathan supported her as her body grew weak with the liquid heat that coursed through her veins.

His marauding mouth was by turns violently demanding and butterfly-gentle as it moved over her face, lips, her closed eyelids, the slender column of her throat. None of the dark, explosive sensations dissipated as his hands slid beneath her brief cotton covering; they grew, entering a new dimension in which all the constraints that she'd once imagined were an integral part of her nature disappeared.

It seemed the most natural thing in the world, and the most exciting, to slide her open-palmed hands beneath his shirt, feel the flat, powerful hardness of his belly. The swift contraction of his muscles and the almost feral groan which simultaneously vibrated in his throat thrilled her.

His skin was scaldingly hot, damp beneath her seeking fingers. She felt its satiny texture as they glided over the hard conformation of muscle and gave a small, guttural whimper of pleasure.

He was beautiful, glorious, the ultimate male animal; and at that moment he was hers, which was what she wanted—oh, how she wanted it. . .him. She moved instinctively as his hands touched her skin with elaborate, skilful precision, eliciting violent, uninhibited responses from her trembling body.

He lifted his head and his eyes were smoky in the grip of passion. They swept over her upturned face hungrily. . . What a hunger! The desire to satisfy it brought his name like a primitive litany to her lips.

His hands swept down the length of her back until he and she were sealed together from breastbone to hip. Violent shudders racked her body with more strength than any fever she had experienced; and that was what this was—a febrile desire, mindless and consuming.

He pulled the T-shirt over her head and it fell unheeded on to the floor. Her camisole was slowly, agonisingly slowly, peeled off her shoulders and very gently tugged lower, freeing her tender, aching breasts. The way he was looking at her made it impossible to breathe. For the first time in her life she took a voluptuous pleasure in her own body.

She moved closer; her breasts, opalescent and pale, swayed gently as the cool air caressed her skin. She raised both hands to pull his head down to her; his mouth closed over one taut peak and she gave a whimpering moan. This need to submit was so unexpected, so overwhelming that she had no thought of rejecting anything he did.

She felt the sudden bunching of his formidable, lean musculature just before he pushed her back. His hands slid slowly and deliberately down her spine, momentarily cupped the soft roundness of her behind, and then she was free. . .devastated, bereft, but free.

'I knew you had a voracious appetite, angel, but even so. . .!' he drawled slowly as, amazingly, he tucked his shirt into the waistband of his trousers and let out a whistle of mock-appreciation.

His words turned what had seemed to the most perfect form of expression into something sordid. Glacial contempt etched the lines of his sombre features deeper; his lip curled in distaste and he actually brushed his trousers with one hand—as though he was brushing off the taint of her, she thought with numb incomprehension.

The sudden rejection and all that preceded it devastated her. She felt fragmented, bewildered. How could all that sensual seduction have been transmuted in the space of a heartbeat into this? Her shadowy grey eyes sought his for some explanation; they only taunted her, and her spine grew rigid. Cold reality snuffed out the last insistent reminders of the rapture which had driven her, heedless of the consequences, into this situation.

'Can't stand the sight of me?'

She felt dizzy. This was some grotesque form of punishment for daring to deny the magnitude of her physical response, the mutual recognition that had occurred the instant she'd laid eyes on him. Yes, he had wanted her—even her inexperience couldn't misinterpret that. But his need to prove a point, to drive home that he had the upper hand, had been enough to make him draw back, exhibiting the sort of control that, as always, seemed at odds with his passionate nature.

Annie snatched up her T-shirt and held it in front of her, a totally insubstantial shield, aware all the time of the absinthe-coloured eyes that were watching her every move.

'As you've pointed out, I have appetites.' She gave a laugh that was entire artifice, and satisfyingly irritated him considerably. The dark brows had drawn together in a fierce frown. 'You were conveniently to hand.'

She'd die before she'd let him see how completely he had humiliated her. Something that had been a glorious amalgamation of the finest and most elemental instincts had been transformed by his cold scrutiny and taunts into a sordid, degrading experience.

'You were at my mercy,' he ground out savagely.

And that had been the way she'd wanted it; the realisation sickened her. 'I hope it makes you feel as happy as you look,' she said sweetly.

Self-control obviously demanded a price. The lines of his face were haggard and his eyes, beneath the hostile disdain, held a restless hunger and frustration which she, with a sudden burst of feminine insight, could clearly distinguish.

'Bitch!'

'Possibly,' she said coldly. 'But I object to being used as some sort of substitute for your stepmother. What's wrong, Nathan? Did you want to sleep with her? I can hardly be held to blame for that.'

The white line around his lips revealed the depth of his response to her reckless taunt. He stared down his patrician nose at her like some avenging ancient god, but still she couldn't be sorry for her gibe. She had to go on the offensive or else he'd drive her into the ground with his relentless scorn and contempt.

'The woman was disgusting, pathetic and vindictive.' The words were ground out and his eyes darkened as he recalled the past. 'When I wouldn't co-operate she told my father I was pestering her.' The laugh was bitter, like a shower of broken glass.

'Did he believe her?' Her fingers, clutching her cotton shirt, went white.

'Not to have done so would have been too painful,' he said slowly; a hard expression then replaced the curiously blank look in his eyes, as if he'd suddenly realised to whom he was speaking.

She swallowed the constriction in her throat, rejecting the surge of sympathy that made her want to reach out, comfort this man. . .her tormentor. 'Why punish me for someone else's sins?' she said angrily, to throw off the intrusion of tender feelings.

'You're two of a kind.' His voice, quiet and deep, vibrated with condemnation.

Annie was shaking by this point, her body seized by an ague of anger. His unshakeable certainty made her want to scream. 'Despite which, you want me.' Her chin went up fractionally and she injected scorn and amusement into her voice. By heaven, if he wanted to think the worst of her why not help him?

His eyes slid over her exposed flesh with insulting familiarity, which, to her intense disgust, gave birth to a surge of sizzling excitement.

'You are the most intoxicating female I've ever set eyes on, but I know you for the shallow, self-centred creature you are and that lends me the necessary immunity. I'll sleep with you, enjoy your body, but you won't suck my soul or my bank account dry.' His voice was thick and not quite steady, and his eyes were filled with a dark animosity that appalled her.

'I'm not like that. . .' She couldn't stop the plea that slipped from her lips. The desire to set the record straight was suddenly overwhelming.

'Don't stand there looking at me like some sacrificial virgin,' he growled furiously. 'I'm aware that you have some very clever wiles but if you think you're going to ingratiate yourself with me forget it. Mutual lust is all fate has in store for us.'

'I hate to disillusion you. . .'

'Under the circumstances, Annie, angel, your protests count for nothing. You'll be mine any time I like and on my terms.'

'You vile, disgusting. . .' Tears of warring anger and revulsion misted her eyes and she hugged her T-shirt to her, rocking slightly as she sought refuge from his insolent stare. Her nostrils flared as she took a deep, gasping breath and tried to retrieve some of her sadly absent composure.

But how, she wondered wildly, could she be composed when standing half-naked, being annihilated by a person who hated her wholeheartedly? 'Oh, God!' she moaned aloud. It couldn't be.

Nathan was eyeing her with suspicion, as though her sudden, alarming sway were part of some elaborate ploy to bypass his hostility. But for once she was completely unaware of his regard.

Only a masochist would do anything as insane as to fall for a man who felt nothing for her but contempt. She had never displayed any inclinations in that direction in her life; love was the steady, gentle devotion she had felt for David, the desire to please, the belonging. It wasn't this wild, voluptuous insanity. Nathan thought she was nothing more than a desirable trollop, a substitute on whom to work out the unresolved hostilities left over from a traumatic adolescence. . .

I won't love Nathan Audley! she thought vehemently.

Her face, pale and naked, like the emotions that flitted with fascinating speed over her features, held him transfixed. He actually reached out to touch the burnished, flaming mass that almost looked too heavy for her slender neck, but his hand, bunched into a fist, was withdrawn and kept firmly at his side.

Quite abruptly the moment passed and her slender shoulders straightened visibly. She managed—and it was a considerable feat—to look almost regal, standing there clutching the rumpled cotton to her breast.

'Your terms, darling?' she drawled, flickering him a look of molten provocation. 'Hardly.' Her voice hardened. 'The only way I'd contemplate sharing a bed with you would be if we were man and wife. A girl has to be sensible. Fun is fun and business is business, and you will always be the latter.'

It was amazing how easy he found it to believe every lie she told him, whereas the truth brought only scornful disbelief.

'I think you're in danger of over-valuing your assets,'

he rasped. His emerald gaze unblinkingly impaled her. He didn't look to her as satisfied as he ought to have done, considering that all his vile suppositions about her appeared to have been proved correct.

His lips tightened and the lines at the corners of his mouth deepened. 'Let me know when you're ready to change your mind; I'm not going to haggle with you,' he said bitingly. 'In the meantime, you can't stay in this hovel. If you haven't already got pneumonia you will have if you convalesce here.' His demeanour became suddenly brisk and impersonal after the preceding conversation.

'I'd have thought that that would have pleased you enormously,' she said with sudden suspicion. His ability to turn the conversation on its head was bewildering.

'The proposition I mentioned. . .'

She closed her eyes. 'I've told you. . .' she began, her voice rising with each syllable, her vehemence rooted deeply, she realised, in panic.

'I'm leaving the country.'

Her eyes shot open in dismay. . . I'm a case for the funny farm, she told herself hysterically, classifying the surge of intense reaction to this information as. . .loss. She knew that the green eyes were fixed steadily on her face so she schooled her expression to remain impassive; the effort made sweat break out across her upper lip.

'The best news I've had today.' Her voice was tremulous, but better, given the circumstances, than she had expected.

'The removers will be at Chausey next week and my housekeeper, while an indomitable lady, is more used to a smaller establishment. . .a bachelor establishment. My son has been in boarding-school, but he. . .' He cleared his throat and curtailed whatever explanation he had been going to give, no doubt deeming her unworthy of one, she thought bitterly. 'The boy,

Andrew, is to live with me here. I haven't had time to employ anyone full-time yet.'

Speculation made her dizzy; why was he telling her this? Had he implied that 'bachelor' was a term in the past tense? Will-power alone made the ringing in her ears recede to a safe distance.

'If you could stay on until I return. . .'

'Are you asking me to look after your son?' The incredulity in her voice was matched by the expression in her wary eyes. Had someone told him of her kindergarten job? His next words dispelled this theory.

'Mrs Gilbert will have her hands full doing that, which is why I'm asking you to take some of the more mundane burdens from her shoulders. I hardly think child care is in your province, is it?'

She had to bite her tongue to prevent the biting retort that sprang to her lips. She suspected that she had a lot more experience of child care than he did! Poor kid, left to settle into a new home virtually alone, she thought indignantly.

'I don't owe you any favours.'

'I thought you'd jump at the chance to stay on at Chausey for a little longer,' he said slowly.

He might have read her thoughts, she realised with a sinking feeling of despair; he had an uncanny knack of probing her weaknesses. The opportunity to stay on was tearing her apart, for while she craved to accept this short reprieve, she knew the pain of departure would only be delayed; she also knew deep in her heart that this indulgence would demand a price.

'You can hardly stay here—it's little better than a shack—and can you afford to go elsewhere? Let's face it, you can hardly rely on your usual charms to hustle a roof over your head in your present condition.' His eyes raked her pale, dishevelled figure disparagingly. 'Frankly, angel, you look like hell.'

'Charming,' she murmured huskily. What a delightful way he had of phrasing an invitation. 'I take it I'm not expected to cohabit with you? At least, not while I "look like hell",' she said with weary cynicism. The aggression was all superficial and he knew it.

Why am I even considering this? she wondered. Her best friend, Jane, would be happy to put her up, she knew, but then Jane had a brand-new baby daughter and enough on her plate, without her and her problems camping out on the floor.

Satisfaction flickered in the elusive depths of his emerald gaze. 'A skeleton staff moves in today. I'll send someone over for your things.'

She made a weak gesture of denial. 'You——'

'I'll be on the midday flight to New York; I'll be away for two months,' he said. 'I'm sure your local knowledge will be much appreciated by Mrs Gilbert.'

'Don't you have a message for your son?' she said, hating his dismissive attitude. There was no hint that he was concerned for her welfare in the way he was treating her; this was all for his own convenience and she was opening herself up to hurt, seeing him of all people ensconced in her beloved Chausey.

'I'd hardly use you as a mouthpiece, would I, Annie?'

She gasped as if he'd struck her physically. Then he was gone and she gracefully sank to her knees and wept. When the storm subsided she knew she hated Nathan Audley; it was that emotion, not love, which had confused her. She was going to cut him out of her life—a total amputation. Nathan Audley was a weakness she didn't need.

Under the circumstances, agreeing to stay on at Chausey was one of the most wilfully stupid things she'd ever done, she told herself wearily. Eight weeks before the serpent returned to turn her out of Eden. Well, she thought, lifting her head defiantly and pushing back her hair from her brow, she might as well make the most of it.

CHAPTER SIX

'LIKE this, Andrew.' Annie demonstrated the correct way to punch the bread dough back into shape and stood aside as he emulated her. She watched the back of his head, bent over his task. This child disturbed her in more ways than he would ever know. For a person determined to wipe Nathan Audley out of her life, she knew that becoming a friend of his son was hardly the wisest course of action to take.

'That's excellent, Drew; just pretend it's someone you can't stand,' she suggested as he pummelled the dough. She pulled a bottle of lemonade out of the fridge and poured two glasses. 'Take a break; that's hard work.'

'You could stay with us; you don't have to leave,' he said, accepting the glass.

The green eyes looked so reproachful that her heart twisted in her breast. Nathan might have been absent since their last devastating encounter eight weeks previously, but when his son continually looked up at her with those eyes it was hard to forget. . .

She mentally blocked this avenue of thought and summoned a brisk smile. Leaving Chausey and this boy was going to be one of the hardest acts of her life, but she couldn't let the vulnerable child see that.

'I've already explained that this is only a temporary arrangement. I have the use of a friend's flat which will be extremely convenient.' And a lot easier than the constant reminder that the new owner of Chausey was living at the end of the drive, she thought. She was never going to make the gatehouse her home.

She was just grateful that Nathan had been out of the country for the past two months. By the time he returned tomorrow her belongings would be in Josh's flat, which was fortunate because one thing Nathan had been right about was the lack of appeal within the walls of the gatehouse. One night there had been enough. Its proximity to her old home and its new occupants would have made it an undesirable residence even if the rising damp hadn't pervaded the whole place with its clinging smell.

'I'll miss you.' The words tore at her heart and she repressed the urge to gather him into her arms.

'School starts next week and you'll make lots of new friends.'

She ignored the constriction in her throat. It was as well that she would be gone before his father returned, she thought. His reaction to this friendship was bound to be volcanic. She could almost hear the nasty interpretations he would list in his hard, unforgiving drawl. She needed a fresh start, not to get involved with any of the Audleys, she told herself firmly.

The child's eyes confirmed his parentage more conclusively than a birth certificate ever could, despite the fact that he was as fair as his father was dark. Those same eyes had unleashed a destructive wave of desolation that had taken her unawares at a point when she'd convinced herself that all there was between herself and Nathan was enmity and lust. The fact was that the only way she could cope with the man was to fight with him, antagonise him; she suspected that, at least subconsciously, she'd deliberately perpetuated his initial misconceptions to keep him at a distance.

She hadn't made any overtures of friendship, but this, rather than repelling him, seemed to have encouraged the somewhat silent boy gradually to confide in her. Quickly the roles his father had expected her and the housekeeper to take on had been reversed—much, she suspected, to the older woman's relief.

It was easy to see that Andrew had long been short of people who actually listened to him and she hadn't the heart to repulse him. He was the most engaging child. . .old for his years yet charmingly naïve. He was obviously lonely and her heart hardened against the father who had so cavalierly uprooted him and proceeded to take himself off globe-trotting.

'That's what Dad says,' he agreed, looking unconvinced.

'You'll see him tomorrow, I expect?' she said casually, watching him drain the glass, her own throat dry. She fell upon the pieces of information he dropped about his father like a starving beggar on food and the fact filled her with self-disgust. 'You spoke to him for a long time on the phone last night.'

The child looked unaccountably perturbed to be reminded. 'I could always live with you, couldn't I?' he said, urgency mingling with appeal in his voice.

Annie made a small guttural sound of surprise but had no time to formulate a suitable reply.

'You two look busy.'

Annie started violently, didn't hear the boy's cry of delight as she whipped round, her whole body reacting violently to this unexpected intrusion. Nathan lifted the child in the air and spun him round. His hair was plastered against his skull after exposure to the rain which had fallen with unseasonal vigour all afternoon. The shoulders of his short lightweight jacket carried the same dark stain of dampness.

If I'd been prepared, she thought, trying to stem the contant flow of sensation that his sudden appearance had initiated, I might feel less. . .overwhelmed, swamped. The gap in her life she'd papered over was suddenly and painfully revealed for what it was: a cosmetic exercise. Part of her had been consumed by this aching loss; she just hadn't acknowledged it.

Annie's heart was pounding so loudly in her ears that she was amazed the boy and his father couldn't hear it. Nathan was watching her over the boy's shoulder, his expression taut. Probably he was less than pleased to find her with the boy. He wouldn't want his son being contaminated by someone whose morals were lower than the average alley cat's, she thought bitterly. What would he say when he realised how much contact she had had? She just hoped the house-keeper wouldn't fall foul of him for allowing her to spend so much time with the boy.

'The place at the end of the drive would be ideal for staff, darling, as you're so peculiar about privacy.' The cultured and rather loud voice dispelled the immobility which had stricken her.

'The original owner has the freehold, Julia.' Nathan placed the boy back on his feet but kept an arm around him.

If the child hadn't been standing here, Annie might have succumbed to the impulse to lock herself in her bedroom and to hell with appearances. Of course Nathan had lady friends. Why the sense of shock, of outrage? He was hardly a celibate, she told herself, trying to resurrect her sadly absent common sense. Desolation and anger made her feel helpless and awkward.

The boy was looking at the new arrival with a look of loathing that Annie, coping with her own emotions, didn't notice until he spoke. 'If you marry her, I'll run away.'

'Andrew!' His father's voice, tight with annoyance, split the embarrassed silence that followed this announcement. 'Apologise immediately.'

With a remarkably similar expression to the one of his father's face, the boy flushed but remained visibly unrepentant. 'No, I won't; I want Annie to live with us.' With that he chose, quite sensibly, thought Annie, to leave the room. She only wished she could follow suit.

The savagery was barely leashed on Nathan's face, which was rigid with the effort it cost him not to explode. It wouldn't take a genius at reading nuances to recognise in the brief moment that their eyes met that he wanted, quite badly, to strangle her.

He *would* blame me of course, she thought resentfully. She wiped a flour-covered hand on the seat of her jeans. 'We were making bread.' She shot a glance towards the woman who Andrew suspected was to be his mother. She appeared remarkably at ease with the situation and Annie, while deciding she loathed her, envied her poise. 'An excellent exercise for releasing pent-up aggression.'

'How kind of you. It doesn't appear to have worked too well for Drew.' The teeth bared in a travesty of a smile were quickly covered by his sensual lips, which compressed into a firm line. 'Where is Mrs Gilbert?'

'I stuffed her body in the cellar.' She couldn't help it, she justified herself as the unruly rejoinder slipped out; it was his bloody superior tone. Didn't he think she was capable of looking after one small boy?

The brooding, contemplative stare was aimed at her head; she could feel his eyes, full of retribution, boring into her skull. The presence of the other woman had to shield her from his immediate wrath; she should have been glad of her presence. Instead, however, she felt her antipathy deepen and crawl up her spine.

The pale blue eyes moved around the large old-fashioned kitchen. It was one place in Chausey that had escaped any improvement. She missed nothing before her eyes came to rest on Annie. The bland smile was dimmed by several volts, but the small, beautifully manicured hand came out. The proprietorial air with which she had spoken was reinforced by her manner; she looked around as if she was mentally ripping the heart from the building. Annie felt like snarling.

She was tiny, delicate, with perfect features made up to perfection. Annie, reaching forward to have her fingertips touched briefly, felt large and cumbersome in front of such a dainty creature. Was this the future Mrs

Audley? Andrew obviously thought so, she thought, dispirited.

'Julia Trent, Annie Selby.' Nathan made the necessary introductions with an air of impatience.

'The same Selbys who lived here at Chausey. You have a charming sense of humour.' The perfect modulation grated on Annie's over-stretched nerves. If this woman was to Nathan's taste, no wonder he had accused her of being overblown, she thought. 'The daughter. . .?'

'Wife, actually. David Selby was my husband.' She held her head high; she'd seen the same flickering expression so often before that it was easy to cope with.

'Tragic, widowed so young.' The carmine-painted lips curved in a faintly malicious smile and she tucked the jaw-length wing of her sleek blonde hair behind one ear. 'I find the old house. . .fascinating.' As she said the last word her eyes were on Nathan, not Annie, and it was aimed directly at the owner, not the home. 'Are you staying long?'

Not exactly subtle, Annie thought with wry distaste. The simmering look was wasted on Nathan, she realised with some amusement as she saw his gaze settle on her pile of luggage. 'Going somewhere?' His voice had a hard, accusing quality and the sort of tone that made Annie want to snap her heels and sketch a mock-salute.

'Yes,' she replied with deliberate abruptness.

'Does that mean the gatehouse will be on the market? You really should snap it up, darling.'

'Mrs Selby doesn't own the gatehouse, Julia. It belongs to her son.'

'Son?' The lashes fluttered; Annie wished they'd fall off.

'My stepson, actually,' Annie supplied casually. You'll have to do better than that if you want to embarrass me, she thought, allowing her grey gaze,

filled with disdain, to touch Nathan's face, which she'd
hitherto deliberately avoided looking at.

The sensation in her stomach, an unfurling flutter,
made her give a betraying shudder. Son. The word
started a chain reaction in her head. The woman was
blonde; Andrew was so fair. The fragile creature
seemed very possessive.

Idiot, she told herself firmly; the world is full of
blonde women who are not Andrew's mother. But for
some reason this logic failed to convince her; if anything her fear grew as the blonde stroked Nathan's
sleeve.

'You really mustn't allow Drew to impose upon you.'
The message in the green eyes was as clear as a warning
siren and totally implacable.

The man leaves his son for eight weeks and has the
cheek to act the concerned parent, she thought with
disgust, her eyes sparkling with anger. 'I found his
company delightful,' she countered scornfully.

'Are you moving far?' No distance could be far
enough, his expression seemed to indicate.

'Oxford; I have a flat.'

'Can you afford it?'

In other words, I can't support myself without
Matthew's help. 'Actually, Josh isn't charging me rent,'
she said with a sweet smile, electing to omit the fact
that Josh would be in the States for the next six months
and she was flat-sitting for him.

'What a nice friend to have,' Julia observed in dulcet
tones.

'Oh, Annie has any number of nice friends,' Nathan
drawled, with a thin, unpleasant smile. His smiles were
filled with an icy contempt which, even though she'd
deliberately sought to elicit it, increased the dull ache
behind her breastbone to a sharp throb. 'She's a very
popular girl.'

The diminutive blonde was looking pointedly at the

jewelled wristwatch on her arm. 'The time, darling.' She tapped the glass surface with one nail.

'Of course; you must be exhausted. . .darling.' He paused in the doorway. 'I'll get back to you, Annie——' the green eyes gleamed with a malicious promise '—concerning what I owe you for your efforts with Drew. I'll just go and fish out my housekeeper from the cellar.'

'Actually she's in the south parlour trying to convince the contractors they can be finished by tomorrow in honour of your grand return, but your premature arrival has rather ruined that.'

'If I'd known the sort of welcome that was due me I'd have been here even sooner,' he observed drily. 'I suppose Drew is sulking in his room?'

'Such insight is stunning,' she said with mock-admiration.

'You see to the boy, Nathan, and I'll sort out the contractors,' the blonde surprisingly suggested.

'Do you mind. . .?'

'For you, darling. . .' With a scintillating smile she left.

'Does she know where the parlour is?' No way could that wiggle be natural, Annie decided, wondering if men really liked that sort of exaggerated gait as much as she'd heard.

'I got Julia's opinion before I made an offer on Chausey. She has an excellent sense of direction, and I'm sure she'll sort out any minor industrial disputes.'

'With her eyelashes, no doubt.'

'Sisterly solidarity, Annie. . .' he chided as she flushed under the irony of his stare.

Every bone in her body ached from the effort of remaining in control. Andrew was obviously right; why else would a man get a female's opinion before purchasing a family home? She wanted to sag, physically and mentally. Her mind, which moments before had been functioning with knife-like efficiency, became a mass of pain.

'Don't yell at Andrew,' she said brittlely. 'He was looking forward to seeing you.'

'I had no option but to leave him, you know. Dragging a child of his age around a succession of hotels is not a good idea.' He raked a hand distractedly through his hair and Annie realised that exhaustion was responsible for some of the lines of strain on his face. 'I certainly didn't get the impression he'd missed me,' he observed, with an almost bleak expression. '*You* were looking forward to seeing me so much you planned not to be here,' he added, turning on his heel.

She sank into an overstuffed armchair beside the Aga and chewed on her lower lip, her expression abstracted, unable to make any sense of the strange resentful expression on his face as he'd made that cryptic parting shot. There was a luminosity in her eyes, a mingling of fear and a furtive, barely acknowledged excitement.

She had known all along that he would be hostile towards her relationship with Drew, but she'd actually fooled herself into underestimating how ruthlessly violent his reaction was bound to be.

Why did he have to come back early? Why did he have to have the beautiful Julia in tow? To oversee the renovations to her new home, if appearances were anything to go by, she decided.

This event certainly put matters into perspective; if anything could jolt her to her senses this should. A brutal therapy, though, she realised, shuddering. To think of that woman being mistress of her home and Andrew... As for Nathan—well, he had never been hers, so that made the pain she was experiencing less justified, she supposed.

Half an hour later she was still sitting there when the door burst open and Nathan entered without ceremony. He strode into the room wearing the same lightweight grey Italian suit as earlier. His face reflected the tempered-steel ruthlessness of his personality and alarmingly his temper was quite under control.

Cat-and-mouse time, she thought with an inward sigh. Then her temper snapped. I've had enough of this. Who is he to intimidate me. . .an arrogant, cold-blooded, manipulative swine with a serious hang-up about women who marry older men?

He was also the man she loved. There, she'd admitted it. . .finally. In a perverse sort of way it made things easier to deal with. After all, what else could he do to her that would be worse than the present situation?

'Twice in one day I'm granted an audience,' she drawled sarcastically. She opened her eyes to their widest extent as she glared at him belligerently. 'I'm struck dumb with the honour.'

Her long, curling lashes fluttered obligingly. He really was devastatingly attractive; it wasn't just the lean, athletic body or the fascinating features with the unusual blend of sensitivity and arrogance; it was the subtle aura he carried with him, an aura of earthy sensuality that no amount of civilised tailoring could negate.

She lowered her eyes to hide the sensual onslaught that she was being forced to endure. If only it could have been possible. . .that he could ever love. . . But no; Matthew had been right to warn her off. She wasn't capable of playing by Nathan's rules without getting seriously injured. Love wasn't a term which he was on familiar terms with.

'Not noticeably,' he responded drily. 'You will not see Drew again. Whatever you imagined you could achieve by befriending him, forget it,' he growled venomously. 'And why the hell did you intend to move out of Chausey before I got back? Couldn't stay away from Josh?'

She began to rise from her seat as he loomed over her, but he placed a hand on each arm of her chair, his powerful thighs an effective barrier. She saw the outline of his strong muscles as the fine cloth tautened, and she felt an instant rise in her body temperature that made her skin prickle.

'This was a purely temporary arrangement and, yes, I miss Josh,' she countered, puzzled by his apparent outrage at her departure. He probably had wanted personally to expel her, she thought bitterly, with his girlfriend an interested spectator. 'How touching—the concerned parent,' she added, raising her eyes to his hard, angry face.

'What exactly is that meant to imply?'

She turned her head as if to ignore him. He dropped down on to his haunches and with one hand turned her chin until she looked directly into his glacial green eyes. 'Well?'

'The only reason your son has been spending time with me.'

'How much time?'

'I didn't have the stopwatch running. The boy's lonely, Nathan.' The fact that she had actually said his name—previously always a thought, never a sound—startled them both. She cleared her throat noisily and let her lashes droop to cover her sudden confusion. 'You left him with an elderly woman who hasn't the faintest notion about how to deal with young boys.'

He had let go of her chin now and she looked at him warily. Her chin dipped and a swath of hair which had escaped the ruthless ponytail she had secured it in fell into her eyes. He reached out and pushed it back, his fingers touching the curve of her cheek, and she retreated into the capacious seat. His hand dropped away, his scowl deepening, and Annie tried to combat the tingling sensation that wasn't retreating despite the absence of physical contact.

'You do, I suppose.' He made a sound of frustration in his throat. 'I'm aware that it wasn't an ideal situation but other than let him tag along with me there was no option.'

'I like him.'

'And you made sure he likes you. All I've had is Annie this and Annie that, and Mrs Gilbert is no better. You've really wormed your way in. What ludicrous line have you fed her about this job in a nursery?' he scoffed. 'Was that to cover your visits to your lover's bed?'

She took a deep breath as outrage spilled from her. 'Eight weeks is a long time to remain celibate,' she said with studied provocation, 'and it was at your suggestion that I stayed on,' she reminded him.

'Not as a nanny. He starts school soon; he doesn't need you. He *does* need some manners, though; he's been bloody rude to Julia.' Nathan spoke dismissively, obviously, she thought, blaming his son's attitude on her own sinister influence.

'Exactly; it's a traumatic experience, starting a new school—helped no end by an absentee father,' she snapped sarcastically.

A dull colour stained the crest of his high cheekbones. 'I am a busy man and the boy was at a perfectly good school; I went there myself. I removed him at his request. I bought this place to be near a good day school. I can't be here all the time.'

'I know all about his time at school,' she retorted, not prepared to let the subject drop.

'Which is more than I do... Agreeing to move him to another school was a whim I shouldn't have indulged. He was far better off with boys of his own age.'

'A *whim*?' she shouted. He was so sure of himself; she longed to sway that inner certainty in his own infallibility. 'Andrew was consistently bullied for an entire term,' she informed him, and watched his expression tauten. 'Did he say a word? No, because his dad thinks a man should cope with difficult situations.

'And that is exactly what he did—he coped fairly incredibly. When he had overcome his obstacles, and not before, he asked to come home to his heartless pig of a father, who, for some reason, he worships.' She gave a sudden dry sob of emotion and viciously subdued it.

He had frozen; the miraculously perfect features appeared carved from stone. 'Is any of that true?' he asked hoarsely.

'All of it,' she said, taking no pleasure now in rubbing salt into the wound. Whatever else was true about Nathan, he cared for the boy. For one instant she had glimpsed pain of such stark intensity in his eyes that it hurt.

'Why the hell didn't he tell me?' he exploded.

'When does he see you? Besides, the fact that you need no one has made a big impact on him. Have you considered the possibility that you're scarring him as much as your father did you?'

'He hated her for saying it, she could see that. The austere features grew remote and hard as granite. 'Who gave you leave to interfere with my family?' The very soft quality of his voice was dangerous. 'Since when did you don the robe of altruistic do-gooder? What the hell would a user like you know? If you try to use my son to manipulate me, so help me, Annie, I'll break you.'

The threat made her quiver; it didn't occur to her to doubt the veracity of the ruthless promise. He had a point; why *was* she interfering, she wondered, when she was aware of all the grief it would bring her? 'I know a lonely child when I see one.' I *was* one. The unsaid words stayed firmly in her head.

'Did you run like a wild thing in these woods, Annie?' His voice was soft, almost like a light caress; though she knew she was crazy, she felt herself begin to relax.

'David didn't mind... Matthew was home in the

holidays. I used to pretend Chausey was mine,' she recalled, a small, sad smile playing around her lips.

His expression hardened. 'And when the opportunity arose you couldn't resist. I don't suppose you ever will be able to.'

The words completely banished her gentle moment of reverie. What a fool she'd been to open up to this man, she thought with self-derisive anger. It was David, not Chausey, she had married; the hero-worship of someone out of her reach would probably have faded like most adolescent infatuations, if starved; but it hadn't been.

For her, the hero of her innocent fantasies had suddenly become less distant; the avuncular interest had become more personal and, most importantly, he had said he needed her—the magic words. . . Someone had needed her. . .she belonged.

The irony was that she never had, not really. In David's world she had always been an outsider, the joke to be sniggered about behind the polite and often patronising smiles.

She had loved David—or at least loved the idea of loving him—but in her heart she had known for some time, even without Matthew's prompting, that he would never have chosen her if he hadn't known his time was short. While her youth and inexperience had meant he could mould her into the sort of person he wanted her to be, the same factors had irritated him too.

She was grateful for all the things he had taught her, but she was glad she could view the marriage in a more realistic, less defensive way now. David had been no saint; he had had his faults, and she could accept that now without feeling an ingrate.

'I got things I wanted from my marriage and I think David did too.' She cast him a clear-eyed look.

Nathan sucked in a sharp breath. She looked so innocently sensual, staring at him with those cloudless grey eyes. . . He stood up, the impetuous movement unconsciously elegant, and began to pace up and down the room, reminding Annie of a sleek, caged wild animal, the sort that stirred your soul but bit your hand if you tried to feed it.

'I'm sure you're an expert,' he agreed coarsely. 'In that field, but not child care. Keep clear of Drew; you'll just confuse him.'

'Maybe it's you I confuse.' It was an instinctive response and his reaction amazed her. He froze, raked his fingers through his hair and turned. His eyes held an almost haunted glitter.

'You'd like to,' he said huskily. 'I'm surprised you're moving in with your young Adonis.' The words exploded from him and his expression suggested that he was annoyed by his own outburst.

Josh—an Adonis! She almost smiled. On consideration he probably was, but she'd never considered the matter before. If he hadn't been seriously attached to a young lady from Los Angeles he could have cut quite a swath through the female college populace. 'Really?' she said with polite uninterest.

'He's not exactly loaded, is he?' Nathan snarled the words derisively.

'He's almost pretty enough to make a body forget that, though.' The provocation was delivered with a sweet smile and she saw him grind his teeth. God, she hoped he was suffering as much as she was.

'Another sucker to freeload off. Or have you got a job lined up?' The supercilious smile made her blood reach boiling-point in seconds.

'I've decided to do a higher degree,' she told him haughtily.

'Another permanent student,' he drawled insultingly.

'For your information...' she began, then she realised he was baiting her, waiting for the swift reaction. 'It beats working,' she agreed calmly, her breathing slowing to a normal rhythm.

The slight quirk of his lips acknowledged her swift change of tactics. 'You passed, then, I take it?'

'It must be all my native cunning,' she responded drily. She rose from the seat; it was difficult to stay on top of the situation when he was towering over her.

Actually, considering that it had been her ambition, her motivation for so long, getting her first-class pass had made less impact than she had expected. It was almost an anticlimax and there had been no one to celebrate with; Matthew was out of the country and Josh's girlfriend had unexpectedly flown in from the States so Annie had tactfully refused his half-hearted invitation to go out to dinner with them.

'So what is it now in the schedule from the grave? Research into some obscure civilisation?'

'How. . .?' she began, startled. 'Matthew told you, I suppose,' she said half to herself. 'Actually I'm switching departments. I'm hoping to get a research assistant post with the social history department.'

It was easy to say but the decision had been difficult; she'd changed over the last couple of years and what she and David had planned together no longer seemed relevant to her. But the feeling of betrayal, which she knew was irrational, was still hard to escape.

'If they can scrape together enough funds,' she added with a worried frown. That was still in the balance. Her small nest-egg was getting smaller by the day, and if she couldn't get this post she'd have to shelve the idea of research for the moment.

'Won't Josh support you, then, while you seek to dazzle academia with your brilliance?'

She gave him a direct look. 'I am quite capable of taking care of myself.'

'No marriage plans on the horizon?' he enquired with an air of bored disdain.

'Actually, marriage is essential to my plans,' she informed him. That was her special interest—a historical review of marriage over the past three hundred years and the impact it had made on several generations of women; the possibilities that this wide subject opened up for her were exciting.

The department she hoped to enter had a special interest in family history, and, if the finance was available, would welcome her as an addition. She had long since proved her worth in a competitive environment; it had been an easier task than proving herself to Nathan ever would be.

He took a step towards her and Annie braced her calves against a small table. It helped her knees, which showed a lamentable inclination to give way. 'Is that a fact?' he said softly, and she shuddered at the threat in his tone.

'I'm sure you can't be interested in my future plans,' she said, hoping that her tone of voice and the tilt of her chin covered her nervousness. His response to her rather childish rejoinder seemed entirely out of proportion.

'I'm taking an interest,' he said tightly, his eyes fixed unblinkingly on her face.

'You're jealous!' she breathed incredulously, then, disastrously, she laughed. It was just so unexpected and the explanation so obvious. He hated her, and he wanted her, and the thought of anyone else having her was giving him a taste of hell.

'Let go!' she yelped furiously as his fingers bit into her shoulders. 'If I scream I expect your girlfriend will come to investigate.' How dared he act this way when the woman he had every intention of marrying was in the same house?

'It turns you on, does it, knowing a man wants you?' he accused furiously. 'You like to tease,' he said, his eyes running over her lithe, lush young body clothed in the sky-blue shirt and denims with insolent sensuality.

'I'm not teasing you,' she insisted, appalled at what she had done. His response was totally devastating and the slip in his habitual iron control hard to take on board. 'I want to get the hell out of your life.'

'Because you're too uncomfortable with me knowing you for what you are.' He shook her slightly and she felt his hands tremble.

'Listen to me, Nathan Audley, do you think I'd have survived marriage to David Selby if I'd cared about what people think of me? You act as if you're the only person ever to think I'm some sort of gold-digger!' she said scornfully. 'I don't care what you or anyone else think about me,' she declared, her voice trembling with passion.

'Are you trying to tell me that your marriage wasn't a business transaction?' His grip loosened.

'That was only marriage to you,' she taunted, at the limit of her reserves of patience. This false picture of her he insisted upon carrying in his head was someone else, she wanted to scream at him.

'Is that what you want?' he asked, a strange inflexion in his voice, his sharp-angled features quite still, unreadable.

'I'd sooner marry the devil; he would have a better understanding of love! Besides, the way I hear it you're already spoken for.' She bit her lip as his glance sharpened to laser intensity.

'Love and marriage. Just an old-fashioned girl at heart.'

'Sneer if you like,' she countered, twisting her neck as his fingers cut deeper into the sensitive hollows beneath her sculpted collarbones. 'Your trouble is you're afraid. . .afraid deep down that you're like your father and one day a face that will be your fatal weakness will walk into your life. So you insulate yourself from feeling anything. . . I pity you.'

'Shut up!' The command, which had been contained during her impassionaed speech, blasted across the silence which had fallen after her words. He pulled her to him almost with the desperation of a man drowning, his hands tracing the delicate contours of her face while his mouth caressed her.

Inside she was dissolving cell by cell; the aching need was intense; it swelled, grew to the point where she felt sure that her mind, already numb and dazed, would cease to function.

He was kissing her closed eyelids, the tip of his tongue tracing the path of a salty tear, and her belly quivered with a hollow, aching need. 'You're a callous bastard and I won't be a substitute body for revenge. Why not take out your revenge on Julia? Or do you have to pretend to be civilised for her benefit?' The words were the hardest she'd ever uttered in her life.

He gave a growl of disbelief and his body, hard and throbbing with the desire she longed to satisfy but had rejected, stiffened. 'You give nothing for nothing, is that it?'

The reflex was too strong to counter, and the sound of her hand hitting his jaw cracked around the room. She took a step back and covered her mouth with her hand, her eyes watching with fascinated horror the livid marks of her fingers develop on his olive skin.

He touched his cheek, his expression calmly thoughtful. 'Woman. . .' his eyes narrowed to slits and he inclined his head threateningly closer '. . .never do that again.'

'Or what?' she countered with mock-bravado. 'You'll hit me?'

'Unlikely,' he returned softly. 'Much more probable that we'd begin what we have started.'

'Rape,' she said scornfully.

His eyes never left her face; he reached forward and took her hand—the one she'd slapped him with. She made no attempt to prevent him, almost hypnotised by the lingering stare.

Eyes on her mouth now, he raised her hand to his lips and slowly, agonisingly slowly, he put each finger in his mouth, sucking, caressing every sensitive nerve-ending. When he finally released her hand she was gasping for air, her breath coming in great laboured gulps. A soft, rosy glow radiated from her skin and her eyes, wide and dilated, stared at him with open longing.

'Never rape, Annie.'

'Get out and leave me alone—I hate you,' she said with deep conviction, the emotion as deep and strong as the previous enchantment had been. 'I'm not spending another night here; Josh will come and get me.'

'Considering you've spent the last two months trying to inveigle yourself into my life, this sudden retreat seems perverse.'

'I was kind to your son because I like him and, to be honest, pity him having you as a father. I stayed on here because I love Chausey.' Her defiant tone wavered. 'It was a mistake. I don't like tyrants and that's all you are. Don't flatter yourself into believing I give a damn about you.'

The green eyes held her own for a moment. 'I'd never do that, Annie. I'm quite conversant with your *modus operandi*. It's the bank balance that interests you, angel, and I do have Chausey.' The glacial contempt flailed her.

'We won't keep you any longer, then,' he continued, his voice coldly precise. 'Feel free to ring your lucky friend.' His lip curled with open contempt.

When he had gone she couldn't even cry, just ache as she rang Josh's number.

CHAPTER SEVEN

JOSH's flat was perfect for her needs, but Annie missed her garden, especially on a perfect September day like today. The clean modern lines of the one-bedroomed flat were a long way from what she was accustomed to. While she could appreciate the pale Scandinavian furnishings and their elegant simplicity, she felt a persistent longing for the patina of age.

She opened the casement windows wide and watered the colorful window-boxes, breathing in the heady perfume of the flowers.

Life should have felt satisfactory, fulfilling; her new job was challenging and stimulating; she had broken with the past. It might have been just that but for one factor: absence had not starved her hunger, her craving for Nathan; it had fed it the way oxygen fed a greedy flame.

In the workplace, without effort she had, in a few short weeks, earned admiration and a certain amount of envy for her combination of self-disciplined application and flashes of pure inspiration. But beneath the serenely composed exterior she was consumed by a relentless masochistic longing that anyone observing her would never have suspected.

She was appalled to even find herself wondering about the exquisite Julia. How close was their relationship? Were they lovers? She tortured herself with the concept. Of course they were... The thought of his hands touching her...anyone...could make her break out in a sweat of sick loathing, and she hated him for revealing this ardent, passionate side to her nature.

Was she Andrew's mother? Was that why he was contemplating marriage when previously he'd been so opposed to it? The boy's comments returned time after time to torture her. She tried to see any of the woman's features in his face, but the father's stamp was in every line of the child. She gave an angry sigh, annoyed with her preoccupation, an obsessive curiosity that could inflict only further pain.

Her letter from Matthew lay half finished on the sofa. Pouring herself another cup of coffee, she curled up her legs beneath her and read on. His optimism and enthusiasm almost leapt up off the pages.

She gave a smile of satisfaction, knowing she could never regret her decision to vacate Chausey. She loved the old place, always would, but it had been a symbol of a fairy-tale existence which in reality had only lived in her imagination. This was the new pragmatic Annie speaking, she told herself firmly.

Her drifting attention was suddenly riveted by a small paragraph; she ran her eyes over it once, twice, three times. It couldn't be true! Anger, confusion swept over her in a tidal wave of bewilderment. The Victoria Foundation couldn't possibly have any connection with Nathan Audley! She reread the scrawled paragraph once more; the implication was clear, though Matthew was obviously under the impression that she was already in full possession of the facts.

The charitable foundation which was funding the research assistant post she had got was directly connected to the Audley Corporation! In effect, Nathan Audley was paying her salary. She stood up, the pages of the abandoned letter falling like confetti on to the floor.

Could it be a coincidence? That possibility didn't warrant a second thought. It was all part of some scheme, some grand Machiavellian design; she was beholden to Nathan. . .

I'd prefer to starve, she thought, giving a small grunt of total outrage. The conniving, devious. . . Tears of temper slid from the corners of her eyes and she brushed them aside with trembling fingers.

All the pleasure she had felt at getting the job, her delight that the Victoria Foundation had been willing to fund the line of research she was so enthusiastic about, had been wiped away. She wasn't even sure now whether any of the projects they had discussed so enthusiastically with her actually existed: the counselling sessions for women who had been the victims of violent marriages, the refuges and the retraining schemes. Her research, they had enthused, could be targeted to dovetail neatly into several spheres in which they were active.

It had all been a contrivance, engineered by their lord and master... He won't be my master, she declared passionately to herself, her teeth gritted.

She screwed up the offending piece of paper in her fist. It had all been so neat, so timely, so convenient, and like the gullible idiot she was she had accepted it as a great piece of good fortune.

The tide of undiluted fury found her in the battered Beetle she'd recently purchased and on the road to Chausey almost before she'd considered what action she had to take. She had to confront him now while she still burnt...let the rat talk his way out of this one!

He was out to dominate her any way he knew how, manipulate her until she was reliant on him. Well, he'd overplayed his hand... Had he really expected gratitude? she wondered incredulously. She was going to tell him in graphic detail exactly where he could put his research grant.

None of her new colleagues would have recognised their efficient new recruit, whose warm smile and breathtaking looks were counterbalanced by a certain reserve, in the wrathful goddess who stalked up to the impressive façade and hammered upon the newly painted door. Oaths of fearful retribution emerged

from her lips as she raised her hand to demand entry
once more.

The door swung open as she stood there, arm aloft,
and Nathan appeared wearing a pair of snug-fitting
jeans and little else. He looped the towel in his hand
around his neck and looked at her, his brows rising in
satirical enquiry. 'I have to hand it to you. . .most
people look fairly absurd with their mouth open, but
with you it just looks inviting.' His tone was smoky,
tinged with that distinctive rasp, incredibly sensual.

Annie's mouth snapped shut. Her well-rehearsed
speeches had vanished the instant he'd appeared. She
had somehow imagined she would have to fight her
way to him through a phalanx of flunkies; his sudden
appearance and his state of undress had thrown her
into a state of semi-panic.

His torso, lean, powerful, was tanned an even shade
of teak. The moderate shadow of dark body hair
terminated in a sharp arrow at his belly where the
buckle of his belt was clinched against his lean waist.
She could hear the rasp of her breath escape from
between her teeth. The sensations throbbed like a
steady pulse through her body, desire a living, breathing entity that all but swamped her power of
articulation.

'I suppose you're surprised to see me,' she jeered.
She almost sighed out loud with relief as the ability to
speak returned. She tried to find a less dangerous spot
to fix her eyes on and failed. Even the sight of his bare
feet made her stomach flip.

'Actually, I saw you on the security cameras. The
way you drove up the drive, I'm not entirely surprised
you didn't notice them.'

'To keep out undesirables?'

'Only selective ones,' he corrected her softly. 'I let
you in.' He blotted his wet hair against the towel and
stood aside. 'A very desirable undesirable.'

'But what am I thinking of, letting a fair maiden on

such an urgent quest stand outside? I can hardly wait to return some of your unique hospitality,' he observed drily.

A guest in her own home; the incongruity was peculiar and distressing. But then he knew that, didn't he? she thought, stepping into the fragrant hallway. It had been easier to accept while he had been absent, but now...?

He had done all the things she would have liked to do to Chausey. If his taste had been abominable and his restoration insensitive, perversely she would have been happier, but no fault could be found.

'Come through and sit down—you look as if you've been running a marathon.' His eyes scanned her flushed cheeks and tumbled curls with a sardonic expression.

'This is not a social call,' she snapped, whirling round to face him. 'Victoria Foundation!' She flung the name at him like an accusation.

If she'd thought to throw him off guard or disconcert him, she was disappointed. One eyebrow travelled skywards as he continued to rub his hair with the towel. 'Is that it? he enquired in an almost bored fashion.

'I suppose you have never heard of them?' she sneered. One silver droplet of water was running down his shoulder; her eyes followed its downward course over the satiny olive skin; her throat felt constricted and she swallowed convulsively, tearing her eyes away with incredible difficulty.

'Did I say that?' he countered.

Some of the anger slid from her eyes as she contemplated threading her fingers through his dark, wet hair. Her fingers quivered as if to experience the sensation. The incident was transitory, the sensations experienced in the blink of an eye, but when she once more met his eyes she could see that he knew exactly what forbidden thoughts had passed through her head. They glittered as green and invitingly dangerous as the deepest ocean.

'Do you deny that you own the Foundation?' she asked huskily.

'The Foundation is a charitable trust,' he corrected her, 'which was originally set up by my company. I have no direct involvement in the day-to-day running of the organisation. I just insist that the recipients of its largesse are in keeping with the public profile of the Audley Corporation. If you wish to know anything further, I can give you an address you can write to.'

'You are an unscrupulous bastard,' she said with deep conviction. He didn't even appear embarrassed, she thought wrathfully. Charity! He didn't even begin to know the meaning of the word! 'Who is Victoria anyway?' she asked contemptuously. 'One of your harem? I'm surprised it's not called Julia.'

This snide comment made him look at her strangely. 'Victoria was my mother, a woman with integrity whose reward was to be thrown aside by her husband for a young trollop. She died before she had the satisfaction of seeing him made a total fool of. But then she probably wouldn't have got much pleasure from it anyway. She—and I'm sure this will seem bizarre to someone like you—loved him.'

'This would seem an appropriate moment to retire somewhere more comfortable.' He ignored her yelp of protest and frogmarched her into the small sitting-room, closing the door behind him. 'Do continue with the fascinating in-depth appraisal of my character,' he said, watching her rub her wrist which bore the marks of his iron grip.

'That hurt,' she complained. His information about his mother still had her flustered and confused.

'Trying to keep in character,' he explained blandly. 'I haven't foreclosed on anyone all day; I like to keep my hand in. Being heartless and callous is a skill which requires constant honing.'

'I'm duly impressed by your wry humour,' she said, frowning darkly. Her wrath wasn't making any impression at all, she realised, intensely frustrated by this confrontation which had had all the impact of a limp lettuce leaf. 'The Victoria Foundation is paying my salary.'

'Congratulations.'

She gave a hiss of frustration and placed her hands on her hips. The action made her cropped top ride higher to reveal more than a glimpse of her bare midriff. Nathan's eyes seemed drawn irresistibly to the inches of smooth, creamy flesh and his heavy eyelids drooped.

'This is news to you?' she drawled sarcastically.

His gaze moved back to her face and the hungry, prowling look caused a badly timed fit of lethargic weakness to pervade her limbs. 'No, Annie, it is not news; I like to keep my finger on the pulse. . .' As he spoke his eyes rested on the pulse that visibly beat at the base of her slender throat, and she shivered as if he'd touched her. 'Did you come here to thank me?' The smile flashed, white and menacing.

'Thank you?' she squeaked. 'I wouldn't work for you if. . .if. . .'

'Your life depended on it?' he suggested helpfully. 'You are *not* working for me.'

'Indirectly I do,' she contradicted him. 'You must think I'm an idiot; I was bound to find out.'

He shrugged his magnificent shoulders. 'There is no secret about my connection with the Victoria foundation, Annie. You appear to be imagining some tortuous plot has been spun around you. I have made no effort to conceal my association. . .why should I?'

He made it sound so reasonable, managed to consign her protests to the same category as neurotic ravings. She caught her lower lip between her teeth and set her chin at an aggressive angle.

'If I'd known. . . I meant it when I said I'd take nothing from you. If you think I'm about to offer. . .' a flush mounted her cheeks as her eyes slid from his sardonic gaze '. . .anything. . .' she floundered.

'You think I arranged the research grant in order to demand my pound of flesh?' Beneath the surface of his scornful amusement she could detect a thread of deadly anger. 'My dear Annie, we both know I wouldn't need to use bribery in order to bed you.'

'Are you denying. . .?' she began hoarsely. His statements had made her drop her eyelids to hide behind the curtain of her long, curling lashes. If only she had been able to contradict his statement convincingly, she thought with a rising sense of despondency.

'You obviously have little faith in the validity of your work if you think that. And I don't mean the job you have in the nursery. . . Yes, Matthew mentioned that when I spoke to him.' Annie decided she'd have to have a serious talk with her stepson. 'You do spread yourself thin, don't you, angel?'

His scathing comment made her vanishing colour flare up once more. 'How I allocate my time has nothing to do with you,' she countered tersely. 'What would you know about my work anyway?'

'Intellectual snob,' he replied, enunciating each syllable with cold relish.

'That's completely unfair,' she protested. Somewhere along the line she had gone on the defensive and he had become the injured party, she recognised, feeling totally outmanoeuvred.

It had been a major mistake to sail in here, in the heat of anger, she belatedly realised. A calm, pragmatic assessment of the unexpected bombshell in Matthew's letter would have proved more useful in the long run. 'I meant you've hardly displayed any interest in me as a person; it follows that you'd have as little interest in or respect for my work.'

Nathan regarded her thoughtfully for a moment before flopping elegantly into an armchair, which was not faded as its predecessor had been. He stretched out his long legs in front of him and, with the reluctant fascination which she seemed doomed to experience whenever she was in his presence, Annie observed the bulge of muscle in his powerful thighs through the close-fitting fabric.

'I suppose that's a fair comment.' The grin that accompanied his words was natural. It knocked several years off his age and reminded her of Andrew. 'I concede you have a point.'

'One sentence is hardly conclusive evidence to support that claim,' she said drily. He had a smile which could charm the honey from the bees when he chose to use it; he just obviously saw little point in exerting this devastating charm where *she* was concerned; she doubted whether he similarly excluded other members of her sex.

'I made enquiries.'

'About me?' Outrage widened her eyes and her bosom rose and fell swiftly.

'You really are a high-flyer, aren't you?' he said. Fingers steepled, his chin resting on them, he watched her with a subdued intensity which didn't fool her for an instant. His eyes were charting every flicker of an eyelash, just as his ears picked up every inflexion in her voice.

'I take it that when you referred to marriage you were talking about your research project. It was an elaborate way to mislead me... I wonder...did you have any notion that, given enough provocation, I'd actually go that far to enjoy the sultry delights of your deliciously sinful body. Marriage!' His lips twisted into a callous, contemptuous smile. 'No, you're too realistic for that,' he concluded cuttingly.

'I can't be held responsible for every sordid interpretation you place on everything I say. The fact remains I won't be in your debt,' she asserted with stubborn defiance. The less he delved into some of her motivations the better! 'Besides, Andrew had already told me about your marriage plans.' She tried to sound careless but she heard the faint tremor in her voice and hoped, without much confidence, that he hadn't. Did Nathan miss anything?

He made an expansive gesture with his hands. 'Fine,' he agreed, unmoved by her passionate declaration. 'What plans were those?' He sounded cautious more than anything else, she noted with surprise.

'Andrew expects you to marry Julia. . .maybe you shouldn't rush him.' Why on earth should I be giving him advice? she wondered incredulously, then realised that for the boy's sake she felt impelled to say it.

The dark brows rose in savage mockery and strangely she sensed him relax. A half-smile tugged at the corner of his mouth. 'Your concern for my son is commendable, if that's all it is. . .'

Why didn't he put on a shirt? she thought, feeling the beads of perspiration break out along her brow. 'I think you're a total hypocrite, trying to get me into bed while you're planning to marry another woman! Not satisfied with wreaking havoc in my personal life, you even have to interfere in my career,' she accused, her anger and sense of injustice increasing by the second.

'When I wouldn't play the submissive idiot role, you set out to prove that I would take something off you, knowing all along that I'd never *willingly* place myself in that sort of invidious position,' she persisted hoarsely. 'You're just a control junkie!'

'Why can't you take anything off me?'

'You have nothing I want.'

'Money, social status—you want both of those plus the financial stability to indulge your undoubted talents in a field where remuneration is hardly sufficient to satisfy you. I would be heaven-sent, Annie. . .' he purred reflectively. 'If it weren't for the fact that you want me, and that makes you feel vulnerable. . .out of control.'

'You are the most incredibly arrogant man I've ever encountered,' she gasped, outraged.

'And you've known so many,' he drawled, his expression almost gloating. 'I can see why you would jump to the bizarre conclusion that I put forward your name as a possible recipient for a grant in order to trade for your sexual favours. After all, that is your stock in trade, isn't it? You trade on your simmering sexuality for items you want, such as financial security.

'Oh, I don't doubt that you have an appetite to gratify, but I think you're pragmatic enough to put that second. As a student of the subject I'm sure you see the similarity between your approach and a good many contemporary marriages. After all, what is marriage but a legal framework to support the same ethos?'

He was watching her with a peculiarly complex expression which, if she'd paused to analyse it, might have made her realise he was waiting with uncharacteristic tension for her reply.

'Historically the theory of romantic love is just as powerful as the economic and social constraints,' she retorted swiftly. His words had stung her deeply, offending every deeply ingrained belief she held and reminding her with cruel force just how disparate their views were.

He gave a laugh. It was a raw, incredulous sound that exacerbated the shattering pain he was inflicting. 'Romance! I can't believe even you are capable of such grand self-delusion.'

Her face went blank, her natural defensive instincts coming to the fore. If he should guess... The humiliation would be unbearable. 'I was speaking out of habit... I was always taught to present a balanced argument, both sides of the coin.'

'But what do you think?' he persisted.

'You tell me—you seem the expert at knowing what's in my head,' she replied, not bothering to hide her bitterness. 'Why did you give my name to the

Foundation? I can't believe you'd do it with no ulterior motive.'

An odd expression flickered in his eyes and he rose fluidly from the chair. 'Your work has merit, is relevant,' he admitted.

His eyes detected the embarrassed pleasure that suddenly illuminated her face. The fact that she could appear so transparent made him angry beyond reason. At some level he was aware that his reasoning was flawed where this beautiful creature, a blend of infuriating contradictions, was concerned.

'Actually, I wanted to illustrate how very simple it is for me to make you do the exact opposite of what you say,' he growled, with an expression of dark triumph. 'You owe your job to me, and before you start dramatically throwing it back in my face remember that the money your department needs will disappear if you do. That would make your departure rather a selfishly indulgent act. . .'

'I won't submit to any covert attempts to dominate me,' she replied, her voice trembling. Nathan Audley was dangerous enough without permitting him to intrude any further into her life; he was encroaching on her freedom to further his own perverse designs. 'I pity Julia. Is she conversant with your attitude to marriage?'

'Your concern for Julia is misplaced,' he replied drily. 'I doubt my comments would have disturbed her unduly. She's a career woman like yourself, and very pragmatic. Aren't you over-reacting to this situation? Or are you transferring the feelings of frustration you experienced in your marriage to a totally different situation?

'Was he jealous?' he asked suddenly, and a step brought him closer—so close that she could see the gold flecks in his eyes. 'Did he try to control you?'

'He had no need to be jealous—or to control me; David was my world,' she spat back.

The narrowing of his eyes was the only indication

that he had heard her swift response. 'I wouldn't blame him. If you were mine. . .' His voice trailed off, a throaty growl, and he lifted his hand and let his fingers trail down her cheek. The soft, feathery touch started a meltdown that began somewhere deep inside her and snowballed.

'You're very free with the amateur psychology,' she murmured faintly, frightened to the core that any moment she would lose control, babble something incoherent and foolishly sacrifice any vestige of pride she had left. 'It seems to me that you want to lay two women simultaneously—me and your stepmother. Subjugating me is a convenient way of doing both. . .the ghost and me.'

His hand fell away as he gave a hard, mirthless laugh. '"Convenient" is not the way I would have described the way I feel about you,' he said throatily. 'Who has taught you to equate sex with subjugation?' he wondered out loud. 'I've been thinking about you these past weeks, happily shacked up with your lover. He can't be doing a good job of keeping you content because the way you look at me, sweetheart, is not the way a woman satisfied with her lot looks at another man.'

Annie felt a strange, light sensation; it was almost as if she was floating; her head was spinning. Was it the thought of visions of herself filling Nathan's head the same way he had been filling her own? It was a bittersweet elation; he hadn't been able to banish her from his life as easily as she had begun to think.

I shouldn't be feeling any of this, she realised, unable to move under the weight of this sudden influx of sweet, warm sensation. Be sane, Annie, girl; get the hell out of here!

'If you put some clothes on it might be easier not to look.' Stupid, stupid! She could barely believe the words that had slipped from her mouth.

He sucked in his breath sharply, the action clearly

defining the concave shape of his tautly muscled belly. She curled her clammy hands into small balls and held them in front of her.

She wanted—it was the height of insanity but undeniable—to touch his skin; touch, taste. Her eyelids felt too heavy to raise, and she let her head sag forward, the heavy silk curtain of her hair brushing her breasts.

'Look at me.' The command was low but vibrantly imperative.

The alternative to obeying him was rushing from the room, not feasible when her trembling legs were taken into consideration.

'Do you want to touch me, Annie? Golden, glowing girl. . .' His voice was seductively husky, just for her. His eyes fixed unblinkingly on her face; she gave a small gasp and some of the defiance and self-loathing vanished from her eyes, to be replaced by a reluctant fascination.

'I. . .' She swallowed and felt the emotion like a solid lump constricting her throat. 'I don't like you,' she murmured indistinctly.

This was terrible, some sort of primitive soul-baring. She wanted to escape but something prevented her.

'Yes, I want to touch you!' The pressure should have diminished when the destructive admission finally saw the light of day, but it carried on growing. . .tearing her apart.

Nathan let out a deep, shuddering sigh. She saw the muscles in his throat clench as though he too was under some insupportable strain. His eyes, those strange, magnetic green eyes, gleamed with a predatory triumph as he heard her admission.

'I've been thinking a lot about touching you, feeling you beneath me, soft. . .your mouth and body open for me.' The compelling words spilled out of him. 'I want to hear my name on your lips; I want to hear you frantic for me.'

His erotic, totally outrageous intimate comments

were propelling her from the state of dormancy that her sensuality had been confined to. The woman in her was suddenly free. . .

She licked her dry lips with the tip of her tongue, drawing his eyes in the process. 'You sound very confident.' Her voice emerged low and husky.

'Do you feel the need to reduce every man to the level of an infatuated teenager? I want you.' His final statement might have been bald, but it was more tantalising than she had dreamt possible. 'You want me and if I don't know what you want at any point I expect you to tell me. . .that can be very stimulating, Annie,' he said thickly. 'I shall tell you exactly how you make me feel; would you like that?'

She was drowning already in just the elusive masculine scent of him; even now, when he still wasn't touching her, she could feel the warmth that radiated from his glorious body. He was talking to her as though she were as experienced, as skilful in the art of lovemaking as he was. She felt her muscles tense in sudden alarm. What was she doing?

Her retreat was neatly prevented because Nathan chose that moment to catch hold of her, his hands on her hips lifting her against him, making her intimately aware of how strong his need was.

The flood of sensation made her feel faint; she was melting against him, her own unsteady breathing in harmony with his laboured harsh inhalations. He tasted her mouth as though he would drain her.

'While you're mine I want exclusive rights.' The thick, passion-slurred words were said in her ear as his mouth sensitively sought the most vulnerable areas, eager for his touch.

Reason and logic were dim memories but his words jarred with her dreamlike, euphoric condition. Fingers buried deep in his still damp, curling hair, she spoke his name, the sound an aphrodisiac for her starved senses.

'Understand me, Annie. . .' She murmured a husky

protest as he took her by the shoulders and distanced himself slightly from her. 'You move out of Josh's place.'

The import of his words still didn't penetrate. 'I live there,' she said, with a puzzled frown. Why was he talking? She was in an agony of blissful expectation. . . expectation of his touch. . .fulfilment of the aching hunger.

'Exclusivity is the only condition I make.'

The sudden chill after the scalding inferno of her desire took her breath away. Her vision was clear; in fact she'd never seen anything with such clarity before. 'You get exclusivity. . .what, Nathan, do I get?'

The mouth which had given her such sweet delight moments before curved with contempt, but she could see that he had expected this query. Anger icier than anything she had ever experienced exploded in her head. 'I'll arrange alternative accommodation.'

'You mean I don't get to move back in here?' she said, pouting with inspired provocation. It seems I'm cast in the role of the slut; the least I can do is get in character, she thought bitterly.

The brilliant, predatory eyes glittered and he sucked in his lean cheeks. 'My God, is that what all this sweet surrender is about—out with the old, on with the new?'

'Tell me, Nathan, what other possible reason could I have for contemplating becoming your mistress? A man who has to reduce every human relationship to a business contract.'

If she'd had any sense she would have retreated from the violence that was evident in every awesome line of him, but she was so hurt she wanted to inflict just some of the pain she was experiencing, and even at this point she instinctively knew that he was too strong a man ever to resort to using his physical supremacy over her.

Intellectually he would show no mercy, though. To be treated like some product with a price-tag by the man she loved had to be the ultimate insult.

The answer was in his eyes and she could see that short of divine intervention there was no way she was going to stop him proving the inaccuracy of her taunt. 'Shall I show you a reason?' he said silkily.

'Don't, Nathan.' His eyes followed the movement of her lips, but the savage, almost unfocused expression in them made her doubt whether he'd even heard her words. She struggled instinctively as he caught her arms and inexorably pulled her to him. He looked wild, primitive, filled with a raw hunger which terrified her even as it thrilled her.

The struggle couldn't last; even as she writhed sinuously to escape him she had already accepted this. Surrender was almost a relief, the inevitable outcome. Then he began a slow, exquisitely slow seduction of her senses, with a delicacy, a sensitivity that displayed how superb his control was. The rampant fury was being tempered to draw an instinctive response that mere force wouldn't have produced.

Breathing hard, he drew away—not far, just a breath—and when their eyes met her total surrender needed no articulation. 'Never try to manipulate me, Annie.' The warning had a steely quality that brought home to her the extent of this man's implacable will. He pushed his fingers into the mass of her burnished curls and let the glistening, silky strands fall, his eyes watching them with an expression of fierce fascination.

When he reclaimed the honeyed sweetness of her parted lips, she gave herself to him with a mixture of despair and elation. The love which had invaded her soul left her no choice but to respond to him. Did he feel as if whatever was between them was preordained? she wondered. He too had been fighting his own battles, she realised, for the first time seeing the similarity between their struggles.

He felt her quiver and spoke her name. It was wrenched from him almost like a pained cry. She needed kindness, sensitivity. But then this ruthless, elemental savage had those attributes too; he had everything she craved for. She twisted her fingers in his hair to hold his face to her breasts. She knew he was the only man she would ever want; he'd carved out a niche in her soul.

'Dad!' The door was flung open vigorously, and banged on the wall.

Nathan even had the forethought to place himself between her and the child. But the few seconds she had were inadequate to compose herself, barely enough to straighten her clothing. She was vaguely conscious of Nathan fielding the child's high-pitched enquiries in a calm, level tone.

I might never be calm again, she thought wildly as she stepped out from his shadow. A small body was catapulted against her and she half absorbed the stream of information being thrown at her.

She slid a sideways glance towards the elder Audley and saw him watching them, an enigmatic expression effectively shelding his thoughts. He was as urbane as ever, apparently oblivious to the fact that he was hardly dressed for entertaining guests to afternoon tea, and she resented the apparent ease with which he could switch off his emotions. But then, as she sternly reminded herself, the emotions involved for him were, at best, superficial.

'Are you stopping for tea with us?' the child enquired as he finally released her.

Annie was spared the effort of gathering her scattered wits to reply by Nathan's swift interruption. 'I thought you were off to a birthday party. . .on ice even. How can anyone top that? Though I expect someone will,' he added wryly.

The reminder brought an indentation between his brows that was a miniature version of the one between his father's dark ones. Annie hoped rather wistfully that his would not be prematurely ingrained with cynicism.

'Must I. . .?'

'I have a previous engagement.'

That was to be her role—fitted in between previous engagements, kept out of sight of a susceptible child who hadn't yet been taught to despise her. The enormity of the mistake she'd so nearly made was too tragic to appreciate fully.

'With Julia, I s'pose.' Andrew screwed his nose up descriptively as he said the woman's name.

'Miss Trent to you,' Nathan replied indulgently. 'Go and change, Drew; they're picking you up shortly.' He gave a sound of exasperation as the boy showed enormous reluctance to leave the room. 'I thought you were looking forward to a trip to the ice rink? You've spoken about little else all week.'

'Will you be here when I get back?' His eyes were fixed beseechingly on Annie.

'No.' She smiled to alleviate the bluntness of her hasty reply. 'Another time, perhaps,' she lied, knowing that Nathan would do anything in his power to prevent that event occurring.

'I'll get Mrs Gilbert to fetch you some tea,' he said as the child left the room.

'You impose on her a good deal, don't you? She must have her work cut out, running around after you and your son.' Tea and biscuits before we take off where we left off! She shuddered, feeling sordid and empty, her wounded heart cold.

His head went back and he regarded her coolly. 'As a matter of fact the whole situation is working out better than I'd anticipated. I feel as if I'm getting to know my son.'

His slow, reflective smile dimmed as he intercepted her arrested expression. 'I've mentioned before that my child's welfare is no concern of yours,' he reminded her. The words were curiously lacking in any real anger. 'I don't know how you've managed to wheedle your way so securely into his affections.'

Could Nathan actually be teasing her? She discarded this unlikely theory.

'All part of my fatal fascination.'

As a fatality of that particular fascination he regarded her with what appeared to be more dislike than lust. 'Actually the woman offered to pick the boy up; she had a dental appointment in town,' he said, an edge of exasperation in his voice, as though he regretted the impulse to explain any of his actions... especially to her. 'I don't want tea either.'

She wasn't going to be sucked back into that sensual vortex that would lead to her self-destruction. But eluding it was well-nigh impossible, she realised a moment later, transfixed by the smouldering green eyes which were devouring her inch by inch.

'Why are you such a long way away?' he asked huskily, his eyelids drooping as he observed the telling way her breathing had accelerated, pulling the fabric of her shirt taut. Then, at the strident peal of the doorbell and subsequent babble of voices, he cursed fluently. 'That'll be the birthday party transport—driven by the motor-mouthed mother,' he added rudely. 'I suppose I'll have to put in an appearance.'

'The joys of parenthood,' she said sweetly. 'I'm sure the caveman look will go down well.' She gave an ostentatious leer while her brain was working at a furious rate. She had to get out—escape!

'Perhaps you should accompany me if you fear for my safety,' he suggested, a slight smile playing around his lips.

Annie quelled her immediate response to this gentle humour and responded coldly, 'I wouldn't want to tarnish your reputation by appearing in front of your respectable friends.'

The smile in his eyes blinked out; he gave her an impatient look. 'As you like,' he said coolly.

The inner corridor led directly to the kitchen. Furtively, afraid of hearing footsteps in her wake, Annie ran down it, her heart pounding heavily in her ears. There was evidence in the cosy room of recent occupation, the shopping bags still unemptied on the floor. But the kitchen was empty.

She gave a sigh of relief. It was amazingly simple to slip out, around the building and into her car. She caught a glimpse of the Range Rover that turned out into the main road before she did and that was all; she was free. Free! She gave a smile laden with self-mockery. If only she were. . .

Would he follow her, and miss his previous engagement with the socially acceptable Julia? She bit her lip and blinked back a tear. He was welcome to her. The memory of the other woman's false mannerisms made her want to scream.

It appalled her to realise how close she'd been to accepting the sort of hole-and-corner affair he had offered her. She was crying in earnest now, great silent sobs that made her shake as she strove to concentrate on the road. He wanted to possess her, nothing else, and how long would that last? Nothing could grow between them from such a shallow foundation. She should just be eternally grateful that Drew had returned when he did.

Gratitude, however, was in actual fact the last emotion she was suffering at that moment; devastation would have been much closer to the mark. . .although her inner turmoil could not be adequately summed up in one word. . .

CHAPTER EIGHT

ANNIE awoke the next morning heavy-eyed and despondent. She glanced at the clock and noted the late hour with dismay. There was no time now to replay all the agonising of the previous night; she had promised her friend Jane that she would babysit her extremely new daughter for a couple of hours while Jane indulged herself in a morning at the hairdressers.

Poor Jane was feeling in need of some pampering; motherhood, she had assured Annie, had been perfected to speed up the ageing process and sleep-deprivation had brought on premature senility. Smiling wanly as she recalled the rueful comment, Annie knew she would have gladly swapped her own brand of insomnia for that which was afflicting her friend.

She had showered and dressed and had a pot of coffee brewed by the time her friend arrived. The baby was sleeping peacefully, unaware of her new surroundings.

Annie patiently listened to the instructions the new mother had already anxiously imparted four times. 'Won't you be late?' she finally said pointedly.

'Are you sure you can cope, Annie?'

Annie gave a sigh of gentle exasperation. 'I don't think Emma's going to suffer long-term psychological problems if her mother is absent for a couple of hours. I'll do my level best to remember which end to feed,' she assured her solemnly.

Jane gave her friend an impulsive hug. 'Thanks heaps,' she said, with one last look at the sleeping baby. 'I won't be later than eleven,' she promised.

'Relax,' Annie called after her, wondering, with a smile, whether her advice would be heeded. Recalling the late-night-party, social creature she had gone to school with, she silently marvelled at the change in her ebullient friend.

She had scarcely had time to finish her second coffee when the doorbell rang. She closed her eyes. 'Janie, Janie...' She opened the door and muttered despairingly, 'Don't you trust me...?' The words faded to a croak as she saw the tall figure of Nathan, not her friend, in the doorway.

'I don't, no,' he agreed blandly. 'Is the boyfriend getting restive too? An open relationship can be stressful when one partner has a more voracious appetite for variety than the other.'

'Go away.' Her attempt to close the door was treated with smiling contempt. She stepped backwards into the sitting-room as he shouldered his way into the hallway. 'You have no right to barge in here, Nathan.'

'Did you really think I'd let things rest as they were?' he grated, his teeth clenched, as he followed her into the room. He surveyed the surroundings with a restless expression. 'What exactly did you expect to achieve by running out like some character in a bad melodrama? Was I supposed to follow you? For a sophisticate you can be irritatingly infantile,' he observed grimly.

'Stop shouting at me—I'm not deaf,' she bellowed back. 'I'm not interested in you or any of the offers you made. I left because you were in no mood to listen to me...you never listen to me, for that matter,' she added sullenly, alarmed at the tremor that had suddenly invaded her accusing tone.

She took a deep, steadying breath. The room seemed suddenly cramped, no longer cosy; this man's restless vitality was overwhelming in the enclosed space.

'If you're holding out for a better deal than the one I'm prepared to give, forget it. I may admire the sleek coat of a fiery little vixen——' his eyes touched the burnished sheen of her hair '—but I'm not about to invite her to share my hearth. I'm sick and tired of your games. I make the rules and the sooner you accept that fact, the sooner we can both have what we want.'

Want! He couldn't begin to know what she wanted...what she craved. 'I'm devastated!' she sneered. 'How tiresome of me to irk the last great despot of modern times,' she bit back. 'You are so thick-skinned and arrogant it just never occurs to you that Nathan Audley isn't the first thing on my mind when I wake up, or the last thing I think about when I go to sleep.'

She blinked. That was exactly what was on her mind, though, she realised with quiet, profound desperation; she was behaving like some adolescent teenager—or a woman in love, a silent voice added.

His fists clenched and he looked at her with such dislike that she recoiled physically. 'Does it give you some perverse kick doing this to me?'

His voice carried such a heavy burden of bleakness that her sense of bewilderment and disorientation increased. What was he talking about?

'I don't know why I'm surprised; I knew you were a vindictive little witch from the outset,' he continued in a harsh voice wiped clean of the earlier raw emotion. 'At least I can be sure you suffered as much as me,' he said crudely, smiling as her colour flared.

'I'm sure you found an outlet for your frustrations with the delightful Julia...the previous engagement, wasn't it?' She cursed her response the instant it left her lips, seeing the gleam of comprehension in his eyes.

'Piqued?' he enquired.

'Not at all; it only seems fair,' she continued swiftly before he had time to continue. 'After all, I had Josh to come home to,' she trilled, with a sweet, taunting smile. It would never, ever do to let him know how much it had hurt, to be relegated to the lowest position in his list of priorities.

Her words transformed his moody, unpredictable attitude into something grimmer. He spoke Josh's

name under his breath and his voice was thick with
loathing and menace. He advanced purposefully
towards her and she froze—as he did when, a moment
later, the unmistakable sound of a young infant's cries
filled the room.

'What the. . .?' A look of confused incomprehension
replaced the glaze of fury which had contorted his
features.

'Look what you've done now!' she said, glaring at
him. The crisis had been averted and she could breathe
again. 'You've woken the baby.'

'Baby?' he echoed. For a man renowned for the
cutting, acerbic edge of his tongue, he sounded remarkably dense.

Annie gave a superior smile, relishing his confusion,
though she knew it wasn't likely to last long. 'Small
things, requiring lots of tender loving care. . . Sorry,
you wouldn't know much about that, would you?'

She moved to the wicker basket which had been set
up in the alcove beside the chimney breast. Murmuring
soft sounds of comfort, she picked up the noisy bundle
and smiled indulgently into the red face. 'Did the horrid
man wake you up, then?'

'You were screeching louder than anything I could
match,' he retorted, watching her with an almost wary
expression. 'Whose baby?'

She glanced up at his face and continued to rock the
child in her arms. 'Mine—is that what you're thinking?'
She pursed her lips primly, or tried to; the sensual
fullness was not designed for such a mean expression.
'If that were true I'd have been almost ready to give
birth when we first met. . . You might have noticed,'
she said sarcastically. Single mother would have been
yet another indictment he'd have loved to add to the
long list he had already composed.

'I might indeed—you were wearing a swimsuit.' He
half closed his eyes as if he could summon at will a

detailed reminder of her sleek, ripe body dripping with water. 'Is it the boyfriend's?'

Annie gaped. 'Don't be absurd!' she snapped. She already felt guilty at having involved Josh in an imaginary affair; she hoped he never got to hear of it. All she needed was for people to get the idea that he went around fathering children. '*Josh* has a sense of moral responsibility,' she said pointedly.

Nathan's head reared as though she'd struck him. 'You have a very vicious tongue.'

She coloured, feeling ashamed of her nasty gibe. Whatever else Nathan was he tried to be a good father. 'I think you take your responsibility to Drew very seriously; he loves you,' she said huskily, and then, because he looked about to reply, she rushed on swiftly. 'I'm going to feed the baby.'

She turned her back on him; that way he couldn't see the sudden sheen of tears in her eyes. She placed the infant back in the crib. 'Still here?' she said sarcastically when she returned from the kitchen with the bottle in its warmer; all evidence of tears had been banished.

He moved aside from the crib, looking almost embarrassed that she had caught him watching the child. 'I can wait.'

'You surprise me. I wouldn't have thought patience was one of your virtues.'

'I have some, then?'

'I was raised to believe that there is good in everyone; you could say I cling to childish values.' She settled herself in an armchair and tested the milk. The baby, its mind focused on its meal, fastened first on to her neck, sucking ferociously, then her breast, not put off by her cotton jumper.

She laughed. 'I can't oblige, honey, but Mum's left you some of the good stuff.' She finally succeeded in placing the teat in its mouth.

She glanced up after several seconds of deep absorption, watching the child feed with the new born's marvellous single-mindedness. Nathan was watching her; his stillness was profound, and his eyes blazed with such an unrefined ferocity that her breath stilled in her breast. How long she stayed thus staring, transfixed, she didn't know.

A small whimper from the baby recalled her to reality and, grateful for the opportunity to look away, she bent her head.

She felt dazed; the raw emotion on his face had been agonising in its intensity. 'I'm going to change her now,' she said as she got up, the child in her arms. 'You might as well go, Nathan. There's nothing here for you.' She tried to keep her voice hard, to stop any emotion seeping out.

'I'll go when I get what I came for.'

'Josh will be back soon,' she said, clutching at straws. Forgive me, Josh! she pleaded silently.

'Good; I can tell him you're moving out. Where the hell was he when you were ill?' he added, his indignation so blatant that she blinked in surprise; was it all on her behalf? she wondered.

She laid the sleepy infant in its crib and turned on him, glaring ferociously. 'I'm staying here,' she said flatly, her heart pounding as a fresh surge of adrenalin sent her nervous system into overdrive. 'You may get away with acting like some despot in your own home, but not here.'

'You never forgave me for buying Chausey, did you?'

She glanced towards the crib. 'Lower your voice.'

Actually, the fact that he now owned Chausey no longer seemed important. She'd discovered that passions evoked by mere bricks and mortar could retreat into the background when personalities became involved. Painfully, by falling in love she'd gained perspective on the important things in life.

'I can understand someone loving a house and what

it symbolised,' he said surprisingly. 'I cared for our home.'

'Why didn't you buy that, then, if you're so keen on continuity?' She would have imagined he would have been keen to regain the inheritance his stepmother had cheated him out of...'Instead of interfering with my life,' she added. She might never have met him then, she realised, marvelling at the fickle hand of fate.

His eyes glittered. 'My darling stepmother had it torched for the insurance money, which ironically she couldn't cash in on because the company wasn't satisfied that the fire was accidental.'

'You can't be sure of that!' She gasped in startled dismay; his casual tone was in sharp contrast to the horror he suggested.

He gave a humourless laugh. 'Don't be naïve, Annie. The only reason she didn't end up on trial for arson was that there wasn't enough evidence. Everyone knew she arranged it—proving it was another matter.'

He shrugged. 'Ironically, she made a fortune out of the site's redevelopment. Maybe that's what she was after all along.' He ran his fingers through his hair. 'Clever bitch,' he said reflectively. 'I don't keep track of her these days but I'm sure she's not starving in the gutter. She could well have been your role model.'

Annie felt sick with anger at the comparison; she didn't see the deliberate ploy to force a denial from her. She just knew that the prosaically told tale was repugnant. The worst part was that this was the woman he had consistently likened her to. How he must despise her!

Knees weak, she sank into the nearest chair. 'Is Andrew enjoying his new school?' It was the first thought that came into her head.

Nathan listened to her polite enquiry and watched with a frustrated frown as her expression composed itself into one of prim remoteness. She had retreated— a habit she had. 'Yes... I don't want to talk about

Drew,' he said impatiently. He'd wanted to draw her out, wanted to hear her denounce the accusation.

'Of course not; he's none of my affair, is he?' she said bitterly. Even if Julia is the boy's mother, she doesn't love him. . .she can't. . . I do! she thought. What have the Audley men done to me? she wondered with despair.

'Listen, Annie, I can't have him becoming too fond of you only to have you drift off leaving him high and dry. . . He needs a mother, not a pal,' he added harshly.

And I'm not suitable material, she thought with a touch of hysteria. He never tried to dress up the nature of his attraction to her, she had to give him that. But to be so brutally reminded of the inevitable impermanence of anything they might ever have together was like a knife being twisted in her belly.

'Are you going to supply him with the former?' she asked coldly. Julia! Poor Andrew would hate her. Was Nathan too blind to see that? 'I thought you were very anti the institution.'

'I haven't advertised yet,' he said, not quite meeting her eyes. Eye contact was not normally something he avoided, but then he wasn't going to jeopardise the opportunity to get her into bed by flaunting his relationship with the beautiful blonde, was he? she told herself bitterly.

'Why didn't you have children?' She glanced up from her contemplation of her fingers, startled by this abrupt question. 'I watched you with her,' he said softly, inclining his head towards the baby.

'I have it on excellent authority that they ruin your figure,' she said with a flippancy she was a long way from feeling. His question had put them in dangerous territory. 'It just didn't happen,' she added as he looked irritated by her answer. Under the circumstances it would have been nothing short of a miracle if it had, she thought with a pang.

'I never knew Drew when he was a baby. His mother

knew that a sure way to up the price was to withhold the goods.'

'What nice women you know.'

'Don't I!' He shot out a hand and stopped her impetuous bid to rise. His expression almost suggested that he regretted his riposte, though why he should suddenly develop qualms about insulting her she couldn't imagine. 'Can't we call a truce?' The lopsided smile was incredibly attractive, and she realised how dangerous a truce could be for her; at least if she was angry there was some chance of keeping him at arm's length.

'Why should we?'

'Because I think we could utilise our time much more effectively making love.' His voice was low, huskily intimate; it drew her like a magnet.

Annie gave a broken sigh. He was claiming her and to her eternal shame she knew she didn't have the stamina to resist him. . .or herself. 'Since you are a self-proclaimed disbeliever in the emotion, I think you should make it clear that we are talking lust here.' His eyes were boring into hers with ruthless intensity; the dark promise of his sensuality was waking all the most inappropriate responses within her.

'Semantics,' he said dismissively. He fell to his knees in front of her chair, a graceful, fluid movement that caused quivers of appreciation in her belly. 'Have you the faintest notion of what it did to me to watch that child try to suckle at your breast?' he asked her thickly, his eyes dropping from her face to the quivering contours of her full breasts outlined in the thin cotton sweater. 'I want to taste you, feel you respond to my touch. . .'

'Nathan.' The two syllables emerged as a hoarse plea, and her sudden movement resulted in her hands digging into his shoulders. . .to push him away. Had that really been her intention? She held on, transfixed by the prowling hunger in his glittering gaze.

His hands moved to the small of her back, arching her spine until his face nestled in the valley between her breasts.

Annie gave a small whimper and buried her fingers in his dark hair; any vestige of self-preservation had long since fled. She was only conscious of the driving, relentless hunger and the aching need knifing with cruel ferocity through her body. She craved his touch, craved pleasure—his almost more than her own.

'Tell me you want me, Annie. I want to hear it from your own sweet lips.' He had raised his head and his eyes, fixed on her face, had an unfocused glazed brilliance. He caught her face between his hands.

'You know I do.' She scarcely recognised her own voice.

The growl reverberated in his throat, male, triumphant, and he caught her lower lip between his teeth, tugging gently. 'You're so exquisite, you make me ache to possess every inch of you. I have imagined you saying that every day since I first saw you. . .' He kissed her open-mouthed, hard. . .staking a claim to the sweetness within. He continued to speak throatily, his breath coming as hard and fast as her own. 'I thought it would pass, but it's matured like something with a will, a life of its own.'

He began to slide his hands beneath her sweater, his fingertips seeking the curve of her breasts, feeling every minute detail, and she suddenly realised, with a surge of feminine intuition, that he had done this in his mind before—rehearsed her seduction step by step. The knowledge was like a powerful drug, a sensual overload. She gazed at his face with half-closed, sultry eyes.

The doorbell had rung several times before it penetrated the sensual haze that surrounded her. 'It'll be Jane—Emma's. . .the baby's. . .mother.' The words sounded strangely disconnected and she frowned as if she couldn't quite understand them herself.

Outwardly the signs of his frustration manifested

themselves only in the trembling hand he swept
through his hair and the pulse that beat in his jaw.

'She won't go away.'

'Wait,' he said as she shakily rose. He gently pulled
her sweater back down and as he did so his eyes
touched her face so tenderly that she forgot to breath.
'That should do it. It would never do for the babysitter
to be caught necking!'

Considering the previous things he had said it
seemed absurd that this should make her face flame
like an embarrassed teenager. She fled from his soft
growl of laughter. He could afford to be relaxed; he
had his goal in sight, she thought with a sudden spurt
of bitterness.

She straightened her shoulders as she opened the
door. She couldn't afford to be bitter; this was the only
outlet of a love that would suffocate her if she let it
wither before it had bloomed. Later she would deal
with the consequences; now she needed him and no
logic in the world could stop her loving him.

'Annie, really, I was beginning to panic.' Jane
stepped over the threshold, casting a self-conscious
glance in the hall mirror. 'Do you like it?' she asked,
patting her new hairstyle. 'Will David like it?' she
continued, with a quizzical look and a laugh. 'Don't
answer. If you say yes I shall only think you're being
polite. My self-esteen is shot to shreds after being
surrounded by anorexic beauticians. I'll never be able
to emulate it myself so behold the vision while you can.

'Annie, how was my angel? Did she miss me?'

Annie blinked, trying to take in her friend's barrage
of questions and comments. 'Am I supposed to reply
here, or is this another rhetorical question?' she said
with gentle irony. 'She's been no trouble—one feed
and change, that's all.' She followed her friend into the
sitting-room.

'Oh, hello!' Jane eyed Nathan with a startled surprise
that slowly gave way to appreciation.

'Jane, this is Nathan Audley. . .' She met the fierce question in her friend's sharp glance. 'He bought Chausey from Matthew.'

Nathan held out his hand and treated her to his drop-dead smile. Annie wasn't surprised when Jane patted her hair self-consciously. 'Beautiful daughter you have, Jane. . .so like her mother.'

Annie rolled her eyes heavenwards. For goodness' sake, not even he could get away with something so corny. She watched with mingled disgust and amusement as Jane responded with a girlish giggle. As she bent to pick up the basket with its precious load Nathan winked outrageously over her head at Annie.

Annie compressed her lips into a firm line and tried to look disapproving, but she had to admit that this lighter side of Nathan was awfully appealing.

'I won't stay,' Jane insisted firmly when asked to have a drink. She continually cast Annie significant looks until Annie could have strangled her, and her hasty departure was a relief in more ways than one. 'I'll ring,' she said, in such a significant way that Annie almost laughed.

'I think she likes me,' Nathan observed as she returned from seeing her friend out.

'I think it's her hormones; anything in trousers has her all of a quiver at the moment. Don't take it too personally,' she said sweetly. Smug, unbearable man, she thought.

'She didn't seem to find it strange you entertaining a man in Josh's flat.' The teasing edge had left his voice.

She took a deep breath and came to a reluctant decision. 'I want to talk to you about Josh. There's something. . .'

'Not now. . .' His brows drew together in a frown. 'I'm not interested in your lovers,' he said harshly. 'And soon you won't be either,' he predicted confidently.

'You don't understand. . .' But he was beckoning her

and almost like a sleepwalker she went to him. He caught her hands and pulled her down on to the rug he had knelt on. The small cast-iron Victorian fireplace — the only item which had escaped earlier renovations — was filled not with flames but with a copper bowl crammed with late roses and honeysuckle gathered at dusk from the hedgerows. The sweetly pungent smell would always evoke memories of this moment for Annie.

Her head between his hands, he laid her down on the floor. She stared up at him, feeling like someone resting in the eye of a hurricane, her hair spread around her face like dark copper petals attached to a delicate flower. Her heart hammered in her breast as if it fought to escape its confines.

'I want to undress you. . .if I've got the stamina.' He moistened his lips. 'Exercises in self-restraint have grown tedious of late.' His features appeared taut with strain and self-control; the enigmatic eyes were glazed with need.

'I could help if that would. . .'

He stared at her for a moment then a fierce, almost feral moan escaped from his chest. It was uncertain who undressed whom, but shortly they both lay flesh to flesh.

She writhed in an agony of delight as his mouth teased and tortured each rosy-peaked mound of sensitive flesh in turn, cupping each breast in his hand, feeling the smooth contours, a fierce expression of primal possessiveness on his stark features.

Her fingers, spread across the muscles of his shoulders, tightened spasmodically, her body savaged by erotic sensations that were beyond her wildest dreams. He was draped over her, his hard frame touching hers in all the right places, a beautiful predator, protector.

His name escaped her lips as he moved lower, his hand and mouth leaving a trail of exquisite arousal in their wake. She gasped, unable to feed her oxygen-starved lungs sufficiently. 'Nathan, I can't bear. . .'

'I could get drunk on the smell of you, the taste of you.' He raised his head and she desperately sought his mouth. Her eyes flickered downwards, feeling the sharpening of every sense at the sight of his magnificence.

He was gasping for breath as their mouths separated, his chest rising and falling rapidly. 'Oh, Annie, I want you.' His hot mouth ran over her neck. 'I'll make you forget. . .' he muttered indistinctly against her skin.

Forget? Oh, Lord, she couldn't forget what she didn't know. Instinct had taken her to the brink but beyond. . .? His hands were sliding beneath the curve of her buttocks, lifting them upwards. Intoxicating compulsion drowned out her surge of doubt.

She felt him against her soft, quivering skin, slick with sweat from their exertions; it was a voluptuous, glorious sensation, but nothing compared to the way she felt as he entered her.

His eyes were holding hers at that moment and she closed her own the instant that her muscles clenched. She missed the flare of shock in his eyes.

The merging was nothing like she had ever imagined; it was a heavy, flowing rhythm which grew in strength and urgency until she cried out, fearing that she would die from the sensation. An explosion of primal potency left her clinging to him as the aftershocks of their lovemaking continued to shake her body.

She was crying; why was she crying? She wiped the back of her hand down her cheek, feeling the evidence of an emotional outburst that had nothing to do with misery, only bliss. Nathan had rolled to one side, his face hidden against her shoulder.

She shifted her weight on to one hip, aware for the first time of the coarse rug beneath them. Tentatively she stroked one hand down his flank. The texture of his skin was intensely pleasing. Her wrist was suddenly caught in an iron grip.

'I think you owe me an explanation,' he said, examining her face through narrowed eyes. He raised himself on one elbow and moved his leg until her thigh was imprisoned beneath the muscular weight.

Her eyes moved evasively; her mind felt slow and sluggish; the languorous lassitude from their lovemaking still pervaded her body. 'I don't know what you mean.'

His lips tightened and his eyes held an inexorable expression which made it clear that he was not going to be satisfied with less than the truth.

'Tell me how a widow, with a string of supposed lovers, comes to me untouched. My experience of seducing virgins may be negligible...'

His anger suddenly seemed incredibly perverse and a surge of anger made Annie reluctantly desert her warm glow of wonderment. He was spoiling everything, she thought resentfully. 'Does this indignation mean you wouldn't have if you'd known?'

His hand bunched in her hair, his expression a mixture of ferocity and self-derision which she, in her distracted state, was blind to. 'I don't think I was capable of making that decision, but I didn't have the opportunity, so we'll never know. I'm still waiting Annie, for some sort of explanation.'

'Or is it an apology you want, because I'm so clueless?' she yelled, humiliated.

She tore away from him and ran into the bedroom. Grabbing a robe, she slid her arms into it, shivering despite the warmth of the sun that slid in through the window. She sat on the edge of the bed, her long, elegant legs crossed at the ankle, and examined her toes with an expression of fierce concentration.

'I'm waiting.' She glanced up. He was leaning against the doorjamb and she could see that he'd paused to pull on his trousers; his belt hung unfastened at the waist and she swallowed, recalling with painful clarity how the hair-roughened skin on his belly had felt.

'What's wrong, Nathan? Are you so bothered that I don't know the rules? No doubt you would have preferred a sophisticated bed-hopper who wasn't likely to get the wrong idea.' She gave a hard laugh and it hurt her aching throat. 'Don't worry, I promise I won't cause you any painful emotional scenes.'

'What exactly would you call this?' he said ironically, and the bed shifted as he sat down beside her. 'I take it you haven't been sharing this with Josh?' His hand pushed into the mattress and the lines of anger deepened on his face.

'Josh is in the States; his girlfriend lives there,' she admitted gruffly. She dug into the pocket of her robe, pulled forth a tissue and proceeded to blow her nose with prosaic defiance. 'I'm flat-sitting.'

He took a sharp breath and although she'd expected some anger the depth of the fury she saw in his eyes as she turned her head was a revelation. 'I suppose you thought it was very amusing!' he growled savagely. 'Laughing at me working myself up into a lather over your affairs, letting me make a fool of myself.'

'Is that all you're bothered about?' she said bitterly. 'The omnipotent Nathan Audley actually got it wrong. You're right—it was very funny—hysterical almost,' she said, her voice rising an octave.

'Sit down.' He yanked her down as she began to rise. 'I suppose it would have been just as hysterically funny if I'd hurt you back there.' He indicated the open door with a nod. 'You wouldn't have sounded so smug then, you little fool.'

'I think you're making a great deal out of nothing,' she said airily, and watched in fascination and trepidation as he went pale with temper.

'Nothing!' he snarled. 'Is that what it meant to you?'

'Good God, you're not seeking reassurance of your competence as a lover, are you?'

'Not from a virgin,' he snarled back.

'Ex. . .'

He let his head fall back as if to alleviate the tension in his neck; his eyes closed and he shook his head as if her attitude totally baffled him. 'Are you going to explain how a married woman remains a virgin?'

'David was having treatment for his illness even before we were married; it made him impotent.'

He stared at her bent head, a strange expression on his face. 'You knew this. . .before?'

She gave a sigh. 'Yes, he was quite frank.'

'Selfish son of a bitch,' he said with such venom that her head snapped up. 'Why?' he asked, raking his hair from his face, his teeth drawn together in a snarl.

'I loved him; he was marvellous to me, taught me so much. I could never repay him,' she said simply. The infatuation had passed but the gratitude remained.

'I'd say you did a pretty good job,' he said with a grimness she didn't understand. 'The doctor said you nursed him at home.'

She nodded. 'Eventually. But first of all we went through all the hospitals, from one miracle cure to the next.'

'That's where the money went.'

Wearily she nodded again. Had it occurred to him yet that if she wasn't a thrill-seeking, gold-digging little tramp there must be an entirely different reason for her sleeping with him. . .? Ridiculous phrase—sleeping, she thought as foreboding sliced through her.

His mockery by itself would have been agonising enough, but combined with the barely contained fury, his reaction to being duped. . . His pride was wounded and he obviously had qualms about having an inexperienced virgin foisted on him. A starry-eyed *ingénue* wasn't what he had in mind at all, she realised.

'Why the hell didn't you tell me?'

'Why waste my breath?' she said indignantly. 'You

have never believed a word I've said to you. You had me sentenced and crucified from the moment we met.'

'Damn you,' he said after a tense pause. 'You tried to make me think. . .'

'I hated to disappoint you; it seemed to give you a perverse pleasure; every foul thing you could imagine I had done only made you happier. Or is that the sort of sleazy woman that turns you on, Nathan? That's it, isn't it?' she accused with disgust.

'And this was the ultimate revenge, was it. . .giving me your innocence? Will you tell your friend over coffee about how smart you were?'

She couldn't believe he thought she wanted to score points that badly. What had happened to the razor-sharp faculties of Nathan Audley, the incisive intellect that left others standing? Why would she have relinquished her restraint for such an absurd reason?

His expression was an ambiguous combination of anger and torment, which, in her own anguish, she overlooked completely.

'I'll leave the boasts to you; I don't go in for that sort of thing,' she said with cold dignity. He had to go before he realised, which he surely would eventually; he was too astute not to. 'Besides, I'd hardly want anyone to know I'd shared your bed.'

What bed? she thought, recalling their passionate, primitive coupling on the rug. 'I think this just about terminates our business.' She tossed her head, sending a rippling mass of hair over her shoulder. It fell against one shoulder, which was exposed where the robe had slithered down.

This would teach her to fantasise; deep down she had nurtured childish dreams that eventually, when he realised his opinion of her was totally false, he would suddenly be overcome by tender feelings. Idiot, she castigated herself. One should always assume the worst; that was the safest course. Would she never learn?

Nathan didn't reply; his eyes were riveted on the soft

curve of flesh. She shuddered, remembering the elaborate primitive dance of sensations he had led her so skilfully through. A skill no doubt gleaned from vast experience; she would do well to remember that fact. Innocence had no value to him; it was an irritation.

'I think I'd better go,' he said, pulling his eyes away with an effort that bunched the powerful muscles in his torso.

'Fine!' she agreed. He was never going to forgive her for, as he saw it, making a fool of him. And what else had there been between them? she thought morosely. There had never been any pretence that he wanted her in any way other than sexually, and in that way she had been found lacking. Angry and rejected, she watched him leave in silence.

CHAPTER NINE

ANNIE tried to convince herself that she wasn't waiting for Nathan to come back—that would have been pathetic, illogical. She could recall wondering how her friends let men they professed to love put them through hell. In those days she had been convinced that she would have told the troublesome male involved to take a hike.

'Why be miserable deliberately?' she had once asked, finding the pitying smile she'd received in return irritating in the extreme. Then, she had imagined what she and David had was the best relationship imaginable; the problem was that her imagination had got more ambitious lately.

It was a torment to sit and suffer. Her body still bore the marks of his lovemaking, and, she realised miserably, though they might fade her memories never would; nor, for that matter, would this longing, which was all-consuming.

It was two-thirty in the morning when the phone rang. She was still sitting, chin on her knees, on the bed; it hadn't seemed worth pulling the bedclothes down. Forgetting that she wasn't going to appear too eager, she snatched up the instrument before its first chime had died away.

'Yes?' she said breathlessly; her heart hammered jerkily and she closed her eyes, her face rigid with concentration. If it was him what would she say? she wondered, in an agony of impatience to hear a voice.

'Mrs Selby, is that you?' The sigh of relief when Annie confirmed that it was reverberated down the line. 'Thank heavens; this is Mrs Gilbert at Chausey here. I know this must be a tremendous imposition but we have a crisis here.'

The feeling of anticlimax she had experienced on hearing a female voice retreated, to be replaced by fearful anxiety. 'Is it Nathan? Is he hurt?' Her lips felt stiff as the words emerged from her mouth. A procession of horrific images passed before her eyes.

'No, it's not Mr Audley, my dear, it's the boy. It's Andrew.'

Annie's surge of relief was short-lived. Tensely, she listened to the other woman's explanation. It seemed that she had called out the doctor around midnight after the boy had been afflicted by distressing stomach pains. 'He was vomiting badly by the time the doctor came,' she confided shakily.

'But why. . .? Annie began.

'I don't know where his father is and I thought you might. . .'

'No I've no idea.' Annie raised her hand to her hot cheeks, wondering if everyone else had assumed that he was likely to be found in her bed in the small hours.

'I don't know what to do for the best. The doctor has rung for an ambulance; he seems to think it's appendicitis. He's crying for his father. . .' There was a lengthy pause. 'And you.'

Annie gave a trembling sigh, her heart with the boy in pain who wanted his father. Don't we all? she thought with bitter self-derision. 'I'll meet you there,' she said, her voice firm and decisive.

'I was hoping, my dear, you'd say that.'

Annie listened as the housekeeper explained which hospital they were heading for. Some of the tension was absent from her voice now that she had shared some of her burden.

Annie flung on clothes haphazardly, her thoughts partly with the sick child, partly with the father. Where was Nathan? She felt anger towards him on the boy's behalf, but it was an anger tinged with concern.

She shook off her dark fancies. No, Nathan wouldn't have come to any harm; he was more than capable of taking care of himself, she told herself firmly. It was hard to switch off, though, and she had a fertile imagination.

Empty roads meant that she was in the casualty department in less than fifteen minutes. She shuddered as she walked in; her travels with David through numerous clinics had left her with a serious aversion to hospitals in general.

After a few enquiries she was taken to Drew's bedside—or rather stretcherside; he was in a curtained cubicle, his face almost as pale as the hospital gown that swamped him.

The housekeeper edged her ample form out of the way to allow Annie to enter. The strained youthful features managed a wan smile. 'I knew you'd come,' he said with such complete confidence that she felt a lump in her throat. 'Dad. . .?' The voice faded and his face crumpled as Annie shook her head.

'He'll be here soon,' she said with a confidence she was far from feeling.

She found herself praying for Nathan to come as she cradled the boy in her arms, feeling impotent. A harassed-looking medic popped his head round the door to enquire whether she was the mother, then retreated on learning that she wasn't. They needed Nathan to sign the consent form—we all need Nathan, she thought grimly.

As if in answer to her prayer she suddenly heard a familiar voice, the one that she would have been able to distinguish amid a thousand others.

'He's here,' she said, relief and excitement warring with fear.

When Nathan pulled aside the curtains moments later he encountered two pairs of eyes staring back at him. He looked at Annie with such overt shock that she thought for an instant that he was furious with her

for interfering in family affairs. Then his face melted
into a smile that made him look a different man—but
still the same man, the one who had stolen some
essential part of her, the one she was incomplete
without.

His attention was almost immediately diverted. He
moved to his son, his mere presence suddenly minimis-
ing the disaster. Who else would a person want when
trouble was on the horizon? His air of quiet command
made the most impossible situation appear possible.
With immense sadness Annie silently left them alone;
she was excluded now—and always would be—from
the magic circle.

She walked into the waiting area and found herself
facing Julia Trent... Oh, God he's been with her. The
devastation must have been on her face because the
artfully enhanced features were transformed by a
triumphant, gloating smile.

'Getting the boy on your side won't help you with
the father, darling.'

Annie masked her distaste behind a cool mask. 'I
only came because I was asked.'

'Not by Nathan; he was with me.'

'Congratulations,' she said in a dry, composed way,
cool enough to make the other woman look uncertain.
Inside, her thoughts were churning, but one dominated:
he had gone directly from her to this woman, the sort
of woman who no doubt didn't need initiating; she
could match his expertise and function uninhibited by
his refusal to express any emotion.

She would have liked to mark the perfect face; the
ferocity of her feelings made her feel nauseous. This
was the woman he planned to marry, she reminded
herself, inflicting further trauma on her nervous system.

'There's no point in your waiting.'

Annie sat on the hard seat. 'I want to see how
Andrew is.' Which is more than you do, she thought,
embittered by the nightmarish situation.

The other woman made a sound of disbelief and sat on another chair several feet away. Her restless twitching during the long minutes that followed contrasted sharply with Annie's self-contained stillness. She had David to thank for her composure; she'd had a lot of practice at waiting, that awful taste in her mouth, for the doctor's verdict, hiding her anxiety from her husband, knowing she had to be strong.

Nathan entered so quietly that Annie wasn't sure how long he'd been standing there when she looked up. His face was drawn; he looked totally exhausted. A dark growth of beard covered his angular jaw and gave him a dangerous, almost piratical appearance.

'He's in Theatre; they think it's his appendix.' He looked as though he was going to say more but Julia forestalled him by sobbing with artistic fervour. Annie saw her fling her arms around him, clinging to him like some parasitical growth. She couldn't watch any more. Turning her back, she walked away.

She was in a state of deep shock as she retraced her footsteps to her car. Numbly she tried to remember where she'd parked it; the entire night was some sort of nightmarish blur; minor details had vanished completely, others kept replaying in her head.

She recalled the tender look of concern on Nathan's face as he'd bent over his son. She was ashamed of the envy she had felt of the child at that moment because he had one of the things she most craved.

And the rage as Julia ran to him. . .she could still taste it as she shook her head to blot out the image of the deceptively fragile figure in his arms. She stopped and looked around at the rows of cars, biting back a sob.

'Why are you crying? He'll be fine, you know.'

How long had he been standing there? She looked up, her expression stormy and defiant. 'I've lost my car, if you must know.' He was so bloody in control. . . She'd seen him loose that tight rein, though, and felt an urge to do so again. 'Some father you are, carousing with that woman when your son needed you.'

The tremor in her voice was appalling, pathetic, she realised, clamping her lips over further accusations, but the words insisted on pouring out. 'I don't care if you are going to marry her. . .if she is Andrew's mother!'

He made a sound of disbelief in his throat. 'Andrew's mother is, at last count, on her third husband. I was the one that got away. . .at a price,' he commented drily. 'It's difficult to believe I was ever that young and impressionable. She has no interest in Andrew.' The expression that she glimpsed in his eyes spoke only of hard resolve, not tenderness. 'A state of affairs I have no intention of altering.

'How on earth did you get the idea that Julia was Drew's mother?' he asked incredulously. 'As for carousing, I wanted to carouse with you, if you remember.' He actually smiled as his tongue caressed the old-fashioned term. 'You sent me away.'

'You went. . .you rejected me!' The rush of relief didn't come; her imaginary history had proved to be wrong but that didn't alter the fact that he had gone to Julia. She was too distraught to feel unhappy that she'd blurted out her suspicions, though no doubt, she thought dully, she'd have time later to squirm at leisure.

He winced. 'Is that how you saw it?'

She stared dumbly at him, her eyes wide, revealing her hurt—a hurt that went too deep for the true state of Andrew's parentage to alleviate alone. The other woman still had a claim to the man she loved. 'I haven't given it a thought,' she asserted stoutly. 'Now get out of my way so I can find my car,' she said aggressively.

He had left her and gone to that woman. . . He was still going to marry Julia, she reminded herself. They had. . . She gasped, hardly able to breathe on account of the vicious stab of jealousy that attacked her.

'You are in no fit state to drive anywhere,' he replied, his eyes on her pale, taut features. 'Give me the keys.'

His voice held the habit of command yet his eyes were filled with deep concern. But she only heard the casual order.

'It has nothing whatever to do with you... Let me go, you bully.' If she let him think now that he could ride roughshod over her he might never stop. The struggle was brief and extremely undignified but her car keys ended up in his hand. 'If I scream I expect several security people will appear.'

'You, my sweet, are too stubborn to ask anyone for help,' he observed shrewdly.

'Give me back my keys, Nathan. What gives you the right to order me around. And don't call me "my sweet".'

Nathan shuddered—clear evidence of the enormous strain he was under. 'Shrew...witch...sorceress.' He gave a strange laugh. 'Loving a person gives privileges.' His mobile mouth curved; the smile was bittersweet and she could only stare suspiciously, not believing what she had imagined he had said, not allowing herself to believe... This had to be some trick, or self-delusion.

'Love is humbug—wasn't that the gist of your philosophy? I think Julia is on your wavelength.' The thought of the other girl sent a fresh wave of fury through her. How dared he come out here, raise her expectations, when all along...? 'Perhaps you should go back to her,' she suggested tartly.

'I sent her away.'

'Amazing what some women will put up with.'

'You think I left you and ran into Julia's arms?' he said wearily.

'You did!' she squealed. He could hardly deny the evidence.

'When I left you I went to get drunk.' He watched her eyes widen in surprise at this information; by all accounts he was abstemious. 'Unfortunately I ran into a group,' he continued wryly, 'including Julia, who were too thick-skinned to know when they weren't wanted.

'Anyway, a message finally got through to me there, wherever there was—I'm still not sure. It was just some bar. I must have switched off my phone without realising it earlier.' He patted his pocket with a frown. 'Julia offered to drive me and since I was. . .am over the limit I accepted.'

'It sounds plausible.' She felt a sudden lightening of her spirit, not euphoria but at least the blackness had thinned to grey. 'Julia implied. . .' She bit her lip as her voice threatened to crack. 'Marry her—see if I care!' she burst out suddenly, everything about her revealing how disastrously she did care, a fact that made Nathan take control of the situation firmly.

'Julia,' he said dismissively, 'is a vampire of a female but a bloody good architect. It should sound plausible,' he added drily. 'It's the truth, and I have no intention of marrying her.'

'Architect! Why should I believe you? You never believed me when I told you the truth.' She angrily wiped away a tear that slid down her cheek with the back of her hand.

A dry laugh escaped his throat. 'I probably blinked and missed it. Let's face it, sweetheart, you've done nothing but deceive me all along. I still don't know how I fell for it. Until recently I was under the impression that you were living with someone. I wanted to kill him.

'I'm guilty of letting you believe your own inventions, nothing more. I certainly wasn't as imaginative as you in creating illusion and I'm damned if I'll apologise for it.'

The latent violence in his voice, his stance made her grow rigid with shock. Julia was nothing to him, she realised numbly.

'You wanted to believe all the worst things about me, Nathan.'

He closed his eyes and his head went back; she saw the muscles in his neck work. 'That's true,' he agreed, and he looked directly into her deep, troubled eyes. 'I came out here to thank you for coming here, not to argue. I know how much you hate hospitals; the doctor who came to see you that time explained that you'd acted as a buffer between your husband and the medics.'

'I'm very fond of Andrew,' she said softly, and with extreme understatement. She was totally thrown by the genuine gratitude in his voice. She felt a surge of irrational disappointment; it would have been so much more gratifying if desperate need had sent him in search of her... Ever the optimist, Annie, she told herself, afraid of what she'd begun to think. . .hope.

'After the mess I've made of tonight——' he ran a hand through his hair '—or was it last night? I've lost track of time. Anyway, after what happened earlier on I wouldn't have blamed you for turning over and going back to sleep.'

'I wasn't asleep.' She ought to have lied, but possibly there had been too many of those lately. He did regret sleeping with her, she thought miserably. He'd looked bleak when he'd referred to the recent episode.

'Are you drunk?' she felt impelled to ask. He certainly didn't look it. Was inebriation the reason for his peculiar behaviour? That, combined with Andrew's illness, would be enough to make anyone act out of character.

'Not enough to swing from the nearest chandelier but enough to admit things that usually come hard to me,' he said with a faintly reckless smile that was almost a challenge.

'That must be the part that says you were wrong—I'd noticed you're averse to doing that.'

He stepped out of the faint shadow and took her by the arm. She could see details now. The drawn, chiselled contours of his face made her freeze; he looked dangerous and hungry, the skin stretched tight over his bones.

'I admit I used my antipathy, my aversion to the sort of female I'd assumed you were, to protect myself from the way you made me feel.' The colour ran like blood across the plane of his cheekbones, and he hurried on almost compulsively.

'I needed protecting; have you any idea how I felt the moment I saw you—vital, beautiful, glowing like a flame, the embodiment of everything warm, desirable and female? It seemed like a case of history repeating itself, my father and then me.

'I'd never imagined I could be that vulnerable,' he said, his voice hoarse, his eyes almost haunted. 'It was a humbling experience. I was in totally alien territory and I went on the attack.'

'You still are attacking,' she said breathlessly. He was attacking her senses with this amazing admission. He looked like a man driven by obsession, a man who had gone past breaking-point and had survived by sheer force of his compelling personality. Had she done this to him? she wondered in silent awe. Had such power been in her hands? It didn't make any sense to her.

'I wanted to crush you. I wanted to prove beyond any shadow of a doubt what a rapacious bitch you were. But all the time things didn't quite fall into place. You said one thing and behaved in another way. I decided you must either be schizoid or you were hiding things from me.'

He yanked her against the cradle of his hips and pushed his face into her hair, breathing in the fragrance deeply. When he raised his head his expression was exacting, hard and implacable. 'Will you say something, woman? I probably mentioned love too soon but I can't believe——'

'Love?' she cried incredulously.

His teeth clenched and his colour faded beneath his

tan. 'Don't reject this, Annie; I've treated you with a contempt you never deserved but all the time——'

'Nathan.' She lifted her hand to his face, realising that he'd misinterpreted her interruption. 'I——'

He caught her hand and pressed it palm up to his lips; they felt warm against her cold skin and it seemed to her that his ardent heart was in the caress. 'Let me finish. I have to explain,' he said, as if he had to work his way through the compulsion to expose his emotions to her.

'I wanted to be able to reject you. I wanted to see you in the worst possible light, despise you. But you kept slipping out of character, and I couldn't understand how everyone who knew you had only generous things to say about you. Integrity is a hard thing to hide and it shines out of you,' he said, with a tone of reverence in his voice that brought tears of joyous incredulity to her eyes.

'At first I thought taking you to my bed would be a way to exorcise you. I felt as if I couldn't let history repeat itself.' His mouth twisted in a half-smile. 'I had to have you come what may.' His voice was soft, steely; a green light flamed from his eyes.

'When you announced that you were moving in with that. . .boy,' he said disparagingly, 'I wanted to drag you off and lock you up.' His expression was raw, primitively possessive, and she felt an answering flame respond within her. . . So much for politically correct theories! They counted for nothing when you peeled away the layers and came down to real emotions. . .the instinct that drew a woman to one man above all others.

'I wanted you to be jealous,' she admitted, lowering her lashes. 'Josh is a friend; I'm very fond of him.'

He ran one fingertip down the side of her face and exerted a small degree of pressure to force her chin upwards until her clear grey eyes looked into his face. 'People are drawn to you, Annie. Drew, Matthew, they love you. You have a generosity of spirit that matches the steel. For one so young you have emerged remarkably whole from things you were too young to be put through.

'Before we became lovers I had already decided I had to have you. . .' He gave an impatient gesture. 'Not just for one night, but all of you. . .permanently. I was going to turn you into the woman I wanted—conceited, I know.' He gave a self-deprecating smile. 'The major flaw being that I already loved you the way you were—are.

'It was incredibly humiliating to realise that all along it was me that wasn't worthy of you. I was the one that was so hung up on the past. . . God, you had reason enough to be bitter, but it was me who was afraid to feel—in case anyone suspected I was human.'

The smile was caustic and his hands, which were cradling her face, were faintly unsteady. 'You have to let me love you, Annie.' He gritted his teeth. 'If I put half the energy into teaching you to love me as I put into trying to hold you at arm's length. . .'

His chest heaved as he sought to control the violent burst of emotion that made her feel as though she'd been buffeted by a hurricane.

She couldn't bear it any longer. His words had filled her with a wild ecstasy that she still couldn't quite accept. But she knew that the pain he was clearly feeling was her own too, and she had the power to extinguish it.

'Why do you think I made love with you, Nathan?' she said. Her quiet words cut short his heated flow faster than any elaborate incantation. Her confidence had suddenly exploded; he loved her, wanted her.

His eyes looked into hers and she didn't draw back from the intimate inspection. She felt the tension suddenly slip away from his body as if he'd found what he'd been looking for. 'I could have died when I realised you were a virgin.'

'Your post-mortem was badly timed,' she told him huskily, her tender heart swelling as she noted the lines of ingrained strain on his face—lines which deepened as he recalled the events. 'I wanted to make the moment last forever, and you acted as though I was criminal. I thought you found my technique not to your liking.'

He gave a harsh laugh of disbelief. 'I think you had ample proof to the contrary,' he said, with an expression that brought warm colour to her cheeks. 'Technique!' he said scornfully. 'What has that got to do with making love?'

'Easy for you to say,' she retorted, aware of a deep sense of relief mingled with no small amount of jealous speculation of the women he had gained such expertise with. 'Everything with you feels natural. But I realised later how clumsy I must have seemed,' she said with a frown, struggling to explain feelings she didn't quite comprehend herself.

'And I was about as subtle——Hell, woman, I wasn't exactly restrained, when you needed a tender initiation. I felt overwhelmed by the knowledge that no man had touched you. . .that I was the first. I was angry that you hadn't even considered the consequences of not telling me the truth.

'Sure my pride took a knock when I realised how much you'd been hiding behind that elusive coolness of yours. I watched the way you smiled at other people, warm, open, yet with me you were so wary, so suspicious.'

'I felt I had cause to be,' she reflected out loud.

He gave a sudden smile. 'I did suggest your name to the Foundation—not that I expected them to be so enthusiastic once they'd made enquiries, and I informed Matthew knowing that it was the next best thing to telling you personally. I wanted to see what your reaction was, and I wanted to keep you within reach. Gratitude was one response you might have exhibited.'

'It was some sort of test,' she said with a flash of fire in her eyes.

He didn't even look apologetic as he met her accusing glare. 'You were an enigma, Annie, and I felt the only way I could learn anything, since you volunteered nothing, was to watch the way you reacted to situations... It was never the way you should have, for my peace of mind.

'Then last night you really threw me the ultimate curve; I felt like some violator of innocence. I know I should have stayed to talk it through,' he said frankly. 'I feel sorry for Selby—having you and never being able to make you fully his. I've hated the thought of the man for so long—despised his weakness at falling for the trap of your beauty, hated him because you seemed to love him.'

'I didn't know what it was to be in love until I met you...you were too much, too beautiful.' She gave a gurgle of laughter at his self-deprecating gesture. 'Go on, you know you're absolutely glorious,' she teased. 'Too handsome, too rich, too sure of yourself, too cynical, not to mention the fact that you breathed fire every time you saw me. I fell in love with you—no logic, is there?'

'I've been aching for you so long,' he said, openly enchanted by her declaration. He wrapped his arms around her waist and hoisted her off her feet. The sensation made her feel fragile and feminine. 'I was so desperate to make you mine, make mine the only touch you ever remembered.' He stopped, his voice suspended by wretchedness. 'Did I hurt you?'

Annie's eyes suddenly gleamed with humour; was it possible to feel so incredibly happy when not long before she'd felt as though she'd never smile again? 'You can see the bruises if you like,' she offered cheekily, the memory of their passionate loving igniting a slow-burning flame in her eyes. But she couldn't stand his expression of self-loathing another instant.

'The fact is, Nathan, what I needed was you; I still do. I hate to sound brazen but I didn't find anything you did shocking or unpleasant; quite the contrary.'

He wasn't proof against such provocation. With a wild cry that seemed to emerge from deep within his soul he took her mouth, branding her as his own with his passion. Gentleness slowly transcended the savagery and when he eventually lifted his head she felt weak with the response flooding through her. He placed her gently back on her feet.

'Nathan...' She said his name brokenly, and the tears of overwrought emotion slid down her face. 'I love you,' she said, putting her soul into the admission.

'Lovely girl,' he said thickly, pulling her to him. 'My girl.' His fingers soothingly stroked her hair, tangling in the burnished mass.

'At first it was a petty revenge, letting you think I was some little gold-digger,' she admitted, raising her head and meeting his eyes before placing her ear against his thudding heart once more. 'You threw me completely off balance. To think that this incredibly beautiful man loathed me... I was mad as hell, and not just with you but with myself, for finding you so attractive. It made me feel less out of my depth to know you weren't so infallible.

'Later,' she continued more soberly, 'it was a defence mechanism. I loved you so much I wasn't sure I could survive an affair; it seemed like the ultimate humiliation to fall in love with someone who only despised me.'

'You put me through every sort of hell,' he growled. He had her, he could afford to be generous, as she was being with him. He was still stunned by the gift she had given him; she had given herself without reservation.

The sound of his voice made her lower lip quiver and she raised her head, her expression penitent.

'Maybe I deserved it, for letting ghosts dictate the present. You were pretty forthright on that subject, as I recall. You seem to think I'm an appalling father, and after tonight I can hardly blame you. Poor kid, I'm never where I should be for him, it seems.'

'Stupid,' she said lovingly. 'You're a great father; single parenthood can't be easy for anyone. He adores you; I can't understand why he thought you were marrying Julia,' she declared, puzzled.

'That could have something to do with a conversation I had with him,' Nathan admitted. 'I did sound him out on the subject of stepmothers. . .only I didn't have Julia in mind at the time; in fact, I'm not sure I even had a mind at the time, because a certain redhead had me half insane.'

Annie felt incredibly light with delirious joy; it infiltrated every cell of her body. She paused, fixed him with a grave, half-shy look, and drew a deep breath; this openness was still so new; the artificial mannerisms were hard to drop.

'Andrew and I *both* love you, Nathan,' she told him softly. The flare of fierce satisfaction in his eyes was reward for her forthright statement. 'The past has given you Drew, so it can't be all bad, can it?' she said happily, snuggling up against his long, lean frame and thinking how good it felt.

He looked down at her face on his shoulder, her hair the colour of autumn leaves, spread over his jacket. His expression was one of pride. 'Do you mind taking on a ready-made family?' he asked, a tinge of doubt in his voice. Her face, innocent of make-up in the dim light, seemed almost childlike.

Then she smiled with a wonderment that held a wickedly teasing quality, and the eyes that looked back at him were womanly and warm; he caught his breath. 'Is that a proposal?' she asked with a small frown.

'The benefits of marriage need not be so unevenly distributed as they were for you, Annie. Is it being a ready-made mother that bothers you? I swear it won't impinge. . .'

She pulled slightly free of him and regarded him, her head on one side. 'This is to be an open marriage, then,' she said gravely.

'Is that what you want?'

'What are you offering me?' she asked, the sultry expression in her eyes openly provocative now.

He gave a sudden gasp. 'You little witch.' He pulled her to him and drowned her soft laughter with his mouth. Annie drank in the musky male odour of his body, and clung to the warmth that seeped from his hard, muscular frame.

'And if I want an open marriage?' she teased, chewing tenderly on his earlobe.

'Bloody absurd term for something that by definition doesn't exist,' he said derisively. 'I don't want to oppress you, I want to cherish you,' he asserted, his expression fierce and yet somehow tender; it made her burn. 'And I want every other man to know that you belong to me.'

This outrageously old-fashioned announcement thrilled her to the bone. 'And you, Nathan—who do you belong to?' she asked, holding his face between her hands. Her fingers seemed very pale against his swarthy skin; she loved the contrast between them— dark and fair, hard and soft; it excited her in a way she was learning to revel in, as she was learning to revel in her femininity. A sorcery had been at work, something primal and beautiful; she was just beginning to appreci- ate how magical the process was, how magical loving this man was.

His hand went to her breast. 'Put me in there, Annie, and never let me go.' His fingers curled against her. His words brought her a step closer to heaven and she realised how fortunate she was.

She took his hand and rubbed it against her cheek. 'Will Drew be out of surgery yet?' she asked.

Nathan glanced at his wristwatch. 'Shortly,' he agreed. 'I suppose we ought to go back. I'd like to be there when he wakes up.'

'Of course,' she agreed quietly.

'They allow parents to stay on the ward overnight. He might appreciate that.'

They'd have the rest of their lives together, and she knew she ought to feel elated, but his words had placed her back on the outside, and her new confidence ebbed. She wasn't selfish enough to resent the time they had to spend apart but she felt excluded.

'What's wrong?' he asked intuitively, his eyes on her face.

She shook her head, smiling to hide her uncertainty.

'We could take turns, if you wouldn't mind staying with him?' His suggestion was greeted with a sudden smile that illuminated her face. 'I didn't like to suggest it, knowing how you feel about hospitals.'

'I'd love to. Do you realise that Matthew will be Drew's brother, in a tenuous sort of way?' She wrinkled her nose and a laugh of merriment suddenly burst out. 'You'll be Matthew's stepfather, or close enough.' Her eyes sparkled with humour. 'Under those circumstances I'd better give you the opportunity to back off.'

'I shan't buckle under the extra responsibility,' he assured her gravely. 'While we're on the subject of relations, I want to get one thing straight from the outset: about Drew's mother. She used him as a lever to make me marry her. I don't think she had me in mind as a permanent solution to her financial plans— the fortune I'd amassed at that point was not nearly impressive enough to satisfy her. She was happy to settle for money in the end.'

He met her eyes and his were dark with anger. 'She was a gross error on my part, candyfloss with a steel core. The only reason I don't speak about her is to protect Drew; I don't lie, just avoid references. But be under no illusion, Annie; she's nobody that will ever touch our lives.'

'I think tonight is the night for putting ghosts firmly where they belong,' she said, her eyes shining up at him like beacons of love.

'I'd like to take you home right now. Make love to you... Does Chausey hold too many memories?' he asked suddenly, a frown drawing his brows together.

'Chausey is just a house; it's the people in it who make it a home,' she replied swiftly. 'Will it bother you that I lived there with David?'

He touched her lips; they felt like warm velvet and tasted of heaven. 'I'm not afraid of ghosts, are you?'

She searched his face and saw love, tenderness and arrogant confidence there. The last threads of uncertainty left her. She slid her hand into his. 'Not any more,' she said happily.

MILLS & BOON

Next Month's Romances

Each month you can choose from a wide variety of romance with Mills & Boon. Below are the new titles to look out for next month.

Fl wer P wer

How would you like to win a year's supply of simply irresistible romances? Well, you can and they're free! Simply unscramble the words below and send the completed puzzle to us by 31st August 1996. The first 5 correct entries picked after the closing date will win a years supply of Temptation novels (four books every month—worth over £100).

1	LTIUP	TULIP
2	FIDLADFO	
3	ERSO	
4	AHTNYHCI	
5	GIBANOE	
6	NEAPUTI	
7	YDSIA	
8	SIIR	
9	NNAIATCRO	
10	LDIAAH	
11	RRSEOIMP	
12	LEGXFOOV	
13	OYPPP	
14	LZEAAA	
15	COIRDH	

Please turn over for details of how to enter ☞

H**ow** t**o** enter

Listed overleaf are 15 jumbled-up names of flowers. All you have to do is unscramble the names and write your answer in the space provided. We've done the first one for you!

When you have found all the words, don't forget to fill in your name and address in the space provided below and pop this page into an envelope (you don't need a stamp) and post it today. Hurry—competition ends 31st August 1996.

Mills & Boon Flower Puzzle
FREEPOST
Croydon
Surrey
CR9 3WZ

Are you a Reader Service Subscriber?　　　Yes ❏　　No ❏

Ms/Mrs/Miss/Mr　_____

Address _____

_____

_____ Postcode _____

One application per household.

COMP396
B